Belle lay in bed, thinking of all the preparations. She had considered getting married in red, but her friends had insisted on white.

"After all," Kelley had said, "you're the only one of us who can wear white in the traditional sense."

Belle had given her friends a mischievous glance. "You don't know that," she'd murmured. Then she'd giggled and spoiled the effect.

A shiver of anticipation ran over her. Tonight she'd spend the first night of her marriage in the house where they would live.

She heard Colt's step in the hallway and another shiver came. He walked in and sat down beside her. She could barely contain her excitement.

Tonight was the night she'd been waiting for all her life....

Dear Reader,

In 20 months Silhouette Romance will celebrate its 20th anniversary! To commemorate that momentous occasion, we'd like to ask *you* to share with us why you've chosen to read the Romance series, and which authors you particularly enjoy. We hope to publish some of your thoughtful comments during our anniversary year—2000! And *this* month's selections will give you food for thought....

In *The Guardian's Bride* by Laurie Paige, our VIRGIN BRIDES title, a 20-year-old heiress sets out to marry her older, wealthy—gorgeous—guardian. Problem is, he thinks she's too young.... *The Cowboy, the Baby and the Bride-to-Be* is Cara Colter's newest book, where a shy beauty reunites a lonely cowboy with his baby nephew...and lassoes love in the process! Karen Rose Smith's new miniseries, DO YOU TAKE THIS STRANGER?, premieres with *Wealth, Power and a Proper Wife*. An all-work-and-no-play millionaire learns the value of his marriage vows when the wife he'd suspected of betraying him suffers a bout of amnesia.

Rounding out the month, we have *Her Best Man* by Christine Scott, part of the MEN! promotion, featuring a powerful tycoon who heroically offers protection to a struggling single mom. In *Honey of a Husband* by Laura Anthony, an ex-bull rider returns home to discover his childhood sweetheart is raising *his* child—by another woman. Finally, rising star Elizabeth Harbison returns to the lineup with *True Love Ranch*, where a city gal and a single-dad rancher lock horns—and live up to the Colorado spread's name.

Enjoy!

Joan Marlow Golan

Joan Marlow Golan
Senior Editor Silhouette Romance

Please address questions and book requests to:
Silhouette Reader Service
U.S.: 3010 Walden Ave., P.O. Box 1325, Buffalo, NY 14269
Canadian: P.O. Box 609, Fort Erie, Ont. L2A 5X3

VIRGIN BRIDES

THE GUARDIAN'S BRIDE

LAURIE PAIGE

ROMANCE™

Published by Silhouette Books

America's Publisher of Contemporary Romance

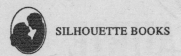 SILHOUETTE BOOKS

ISBN 0-373-19318-1

THE GUARDIAN'S BRIDE

Copyright © 1998 by Olivia M. Hall

This edition published by arrangement with Harlequin Books S.A.

Printed in U.S.A.

LAURIE PAIGE

was recently presented with the *Affaire de Coeur* Readers' Choice Silver Pen Award for Favorite Contemporary Author. In addition, she was a 1994 Romance Writers of America (RITA) finalist for Best Traditional Romance for her book *Sally's Beau*. She reports romance is blooming in her part of northern California. With the birth of her second grandson, she finds herself madly in love with three wonderful males— "all hero material." So far, her husband hasn't complained about the other men in her life.

Dear Reader,

Cupid has been working overtime this past year. My calendar has been filled with wedding dates—nieces and nephews, friends' children, neighbors. Winter weddings, summer weddings. Afternoon and evening ones. One wedding was in a rose garden, another at an arboretum where the vinca had been mowed to an inch high in early spring, so that it formed a carpet of purple blooms for the wedding ceremony. One bride wore red because that is the color of good luck in her culture. I cried at all of them.

The mother in me wants to advise, "The beginning can determine how you will get on. If something really bothers you, explain that to your partner and seek a solution. Don't wait until an explosion occurs."

The writer would like to plot out their lives and their children's lives, to plan for emergencies and to schedule in the highlights to keep things perking along at an interesting pace.

The romantic wants to tell the couple, "Listen, the things you love about each other right now, at this magic moment, will still be there five years from now and ten years and fifteen...but you might have to search for them. That quirky sense of humor, the love of three-hankie movies, the pleasure in long walks at twilight, these can get buried under dental appointments, soccer practice and Thanksgiving dinners. Don't forget why you love each other."

All this is wonderful advice, but I've noticed that the real couples I know act just like my fictional ones—they totally ignore what I think and do their own thing!

Warm regards,

Laurie Paige

Chapter One

Belle woke with a start then realized she wasn't having a nightmare. There really was an octopus on her. She could count several arms, legs, whatevers, between her and freedom. She used several expressions picked up from her early days when her father had been an oil-field roustabout while she fought off the monster.

"Will you shut up!" an angry male voice demanded.

"Colt? Is that you?" she asked.

"Who the hell would you expect it to be?"

She threw her arms around him and squeezed as hard as she could. She was so glad to see him...well, hear him. She could only make out a dark shape sprawled out over her. He felt odd, though.

"Get your hands off me," a feminine voice demanded.

Belle realized they weren't alone. She laughed in

relief. "Whew, for a minute there I thought you'd grown some strange protuberances," she confided to Colt.

His cheek was against hers. She knew it was him because she could smell the familiar spicy scent of his aftershave. Her heart gave a little kick of joy. "Do you think you could move? I can't breathe."

There was a struggle above her, then the weight lifted and separated itself into two shadows against the lights of the skyline. She saw the larger shadow move, then heard him fumble with the lamp switch.

The light came on.

She stared into two pairs of eyes, one gray—that was Colt—the other blue—that was some strange female looking at her as if she were a spotted lizard who'd invaded her bed.

"Who are you?" the woman demanded. "Colt, I think you should call the police. She obviously broke in—"

"No, I didn't. Colt gave me a key," Belle said, setting the snooty female straight. There was nothing that got her dander up more than snootiness. "Years ago."

She didn't mention that he'd also thrown her out when she'd tried to seduce him. Well, not exactly seduce. She'd thought the feeling was mutual, that he'd wanted her as much as she'd wanted him.

At seventeen, she'd had a lot to learn about men and women. Looking at Colt and the gorgeous female who exuded sophisticated haughtiness, she thought she might have a few lessons to go even though she was three years older and a lot wiser than she'd been back then.

The woman was obviously cold, calculating and mean-hearted, wanting to put her in jail without knowing the reasons she was there. Belle couldn't figure out why Colt would want to date her even if she was as beautiful as a fashion doll decked out for high society.

"Did you come here to put on a strip show?" Colt asked, not at all glad to see her.

Seeing his lips tighten angrily as his icy gaze skimmed along her legs, Belle realized her nightshirt was rucked up above her high-cut briefs. She yanked the cotton knit down over her thighs.

"It was your fault," she said, defending herself. "If you and your sex-crazed girlfriend hadn't fallen on me like an octopus in the throes of passion, I wouldn't have had to fight you off—"

"Well, really," the girlfriend said.

"Enough," Colt said in a controlled roar.

Belle shut up and gazed at him, her eyes as big and innocent as she could make them. She tried to summon a tear or two, but all she could think of was how handsome he looked with his charcoal gray eyes and coal black hair, his muscular leanness and sinewy strength. Once she'd thought no one could match him for masculine beauty. Once, when she'd been young and foolish.

The society doll smoothed her hair and gave Belle a disdainful once-over. "Really, Colt, I didn't know you were drawn to the Lolita type."

The amused, condescending tone irked Belle. "I'm not a child. I'm twenty, almost twenty-one. In four more months," she added truthfully.

"When did you get here?" he demanded.

"Around midnight. I drove for two days straight. I, umm, thought I'd visit with you for a while—"

"Absolutely not," the other woman stated. At Colt's sharp glance, she backed off. "Unless she's a relative?"

"No." Belle and Colt spoke together. Colt did a quick introduction, "Marsha Montbatten, Belle Glamorgan."

"Colt, it really isn't appropriate for her to be here," the woman advised, her expression filling with concern as if her only interest was to protect him.

Belle judged her to be around thirty. She was dressed in a black silk outfit cut low in the front and high in a provocative slit on the side. Jewels sparkled at her ears and throat. Probably real. A white lacy stole lay on the floor near the door in a seductive heap.

Materialistic, Belle added to the list of the other female's attributes. The woman was obviously a casual date. Colt wouldn't fall for a brittle society doll.

Belle relaxed. For a minute there, she had felt a spasm of fear that he'd fallen in love, but, for a bachelor, bringing a female to his apartment didn't necessarily mean anything other than purely sexual interest.

Looking at the hard set of Colt's jaw, she realized he agreed with the blond beauty. He wasn't glad to see her, and she definitely wasn't welcome in his home.

A hot, achy feeling washed over her like a caldron of boiling water. She tugged at the nightshirt which had slipped halfway up her thighs again. "I didn't think...I mean, I've always come here...I'll leave right away,'' she said with as much dignity as she could manage.

"No," Colt said on a kinder note.

Belle and the other woman stared at him.

"You can stay here. For a while." He stripped off his tie and jacket. "Marsha, I'll call a cab for you."

"You're going to allow her to stay?" Marsha demanded.

Belle watched the couple with interest, her inner calm restored now that he'd okayed her visit.

"Belle's father was my business partner. I was named her guardian in his will. Belle is... There's a problem we need to sort out. I'll see you tomorrow for lunch."

"Oh, you're her guardian." This seemed to pacify the beauteous Marsha. She gave Belle an amused glance one would bestow on a bothersome child, then smiled in sympathy and understanding at Colt. "All right. Pick me up at one. We'll talk then."

"Fine." He ushered the beauty out.

Belle's spirits sank lower at hearing herself described as a problem. Colt evidently thought she was a major headache, judging by the expression on his face. She hadn't really expected a warm welcome from him, but it would have been nice to be greeted as a friend rather than a nuisance. She'd missed him.

She pulled her knees to her chest, making sure the shirt covered her legs completely and waited glumly while he got rid of his date. She had a feeling he wasn't going to be very receptive to her brilliant idea.

Colter McKinnon was a man who guarded his privacy. He'd made it clear the last time she'd barged in that she wouldn't be welcome in the future without an invitation. But things were different now. She was almost twenty-one. She wouldn't be ordered about like a kid anymore. She had ideas of her own.

"In here," Colt said curtly, striding through the elegant black-lacquered entrance door and locking the dead bolt behind him.

Belle followed him into the modern kitchen, gathering her courage and her arguments in hand. A sinking feeling invaded her middle. What if he wouldn't let her stay after that fiasco three years ago?

When he'd bought the luxurious condo, shortly before she graduated from high school, she'd thought it was because he was ready for a home and family...with her.

Upon graduation, she'd gone to him and told him that she was ready, too. He'd quickly disabused her of any romantic notions she'd harbored. He'd made it clear his interest was in *women,* not untried girls such as herself. She'd had to swallow the hurt, pull her ragged pride around her and pretend she'd been joking.

That summer she'd been glad her father had sent her off to Europe on one of the endless educational trips she took with old-maid teachers to improve her mind. Six weeks later, she'd returned home in time to attend her father's funeral. He'd died of a heart attack two days before her arrival.

Harold Glamorgan, a big red-headed Texan of Irish descent who'd liked his tot of whiskey, his after-dinner cigar, his steak and potatoes, dead? Unbelievable.

For a moment, she recalled the times he'd come in

from the oil fields, dirty and exuberant, with a hug for her and her mother....

She pushed away the memories of her loss, the sudden fear of being alone, the unexpected longing for the mother who had died when she was twelve—and the gaunt realization she was unwanted by anyone in the world.

Colt had once been her champion. No more. After her father's death, he'd changed, becoming more demanding than her father had been, questioning her about the classes at the all-female college her dad had insisted she attend, checking her grades and frowning if they weren't up to his standards, exhorting her to do better, especially in the business courses she detested.

"If I remember correctly—and I've had no indications of senility yet—you're supposed to be on a tour of Greece."

"I didn't go."

"Obviously." He leveled a hard stare at her, then set about putting on a pot of coffee. "Explain yourself."

The plans that had seemed so logical when she headed for Dallas instead of New York and a plane to Athens now seemed feeble and juvenile.

"I'm going to be twenty-one in October," she reminded him. "I'll come into my inheritance then."

He folded his arms across his chest while the coffee gurgled cheerily, a sound at odds with the atmosphere in the comfortable kitchen with its green-and-white floor, white counter and mellow oak cabinets. It was her favorite room in the modern penthouse, which she thought was a cold place.

"*If* I approve the transfer of funds from the trust," he reminded her. "I can hold them until you're twenty-five."

She could read nothing from his expression. "I know. The easiest way to learn is by doing, so I thought you could teach me what I need to know."

"In four months?"

"Not entirely, but it would be a start."

She avoided his uncompromising frown and stared at the herbs lining the window over the sink. The tiny ceramic pots had the name of the plant written in the glaze. They had been a house-warming gift from her. She noted the leaves looked healthy, indicating Colt took good care of them.

"You have one year of college to go. Don't you think you should delay your leap into the corporate world until you finish?"

"You and Dad didn't go to college." Seeing that argument wasn't going to sway him, she tried another. "Why can't I go to school here and learn the business at the same time? That makes sense."

"Your father—"

"Wanted me to attend the school in Virginia. I've done that. I want to come home, Colt. I'm..."

Lonely? Tired? Unhappy? Choose one.

The odd thought produced the tears she'd wished for earlier. She blinked them away while he poured two cups of coffee and joined her at the table. He put a tin of cookies on the oak table between them.

Give the child a cookie and a pat on the head, then send her on her way?

The stubbornness inherited from her father surfaced. She was not going to be dissuaded by threats or treats.

"The daughter of Hal Glamorgan giving up?" The note of disbelief in his baritone voice was deliberate. "Have you flunked out?"

"No." She ignored the cookies and took a sip of the strong brew, then grimaced. Colt made the worst coffee. "I've hardly been in Texas, much less Dallas, since Mom died. I've been sent to boarding school or camp or on world tours for eight years. When do I get to have a place of my own that isn't a dorm or hotel room?"

A flicker of emotion passed through his eyes, too quick to read. However, it looked as if he might be softening toward her. He'd seemed pretty angry when he'd first made the coffee and ordered her to explain her presence. Now he looked thoughtful.

She glanced at him, her spirits rising slightly. They immediately plummeted again. His eyes were still the same icy gray they'd been when he'd turned on the light and discovered her in his home.

"When you grow up?" he suggested coolly.

She didn't dignify the remark by protesting.

He sighed and ran a hand through his hair. The cowlick to the left of his forehead caused a dark lock to spring forward in an arc as soon as he released it. It saved his sharply angled face from harshness and lent a certain charm to his decidedly masculine features when he smiled.

Which was seldom when she was around.

"Why did you come here?" he asked.

"I didn't have anyplace else to go," she said without thinking, surprised that he would ask. Her dad had sold the ranch and the home she'd come to love after her mom died.

"You don't have any girlfriends who would take you in?"

She hadn't considered anyone else. "No."

"You were in a sorority."

"Everyone was in one. What else was there to do at an all-female college out in the boonies?"

She didn't mention the dances to which the guys from the university were invited. She'd hated the fake social occasions, the giggles of the other girls as they dressed, their talk focused on the coming evening.

All the fraternity guys had wanted to do was get the girls outside in the dark. Their kisses had been repulsive—wet and intrusive. Neanderthals. Of course, the Neanderthals' fathers were the richest men in the country—

"Belle," Colt said sharply.

"Besides, most of them were snobs. Just like your girlfriend—" She stopped. It probably wasn't a good idea to criticize his taste in women, especially when she'd come to ask a favor.

"Thanks very much. That's the woman I was planning on asking to marry me tonight."

"Colt, no," she said, horrified and somehow hurt that he would think of marriage to someone so cold. "You can't... She was awful...." At the flash of fury in his eyes, she tried to recover. "Well, actually, not awful...or maybe not too awful..."

At his sarcastic glance, she realized she was digging herself in deeper. And he was going to let her.

"She's very beautiful," she offered.

"Yes, she is."

"Are you very much in love with her?"

His eyebrows shot up, then his eyes narrowed. He was like a desert rattler. He didn't like anyone too close. A look from those frigid gray eyes was enough to turn most people off.

Of course, most people didn't care about him and his happiness. She did. In spite of what had happened when he'd told her not to come there again, she couldn't forget that he'd once been her best friend.

"Love is a fool's game," he informed her. "Haven't you learned that yet?"

She shook her head. "Why would you want to marry someone if you don't love her?"

"Her father has connections. She's a good hostess. We make a good team." His smile dared her to make something of his cynical remark.

"That's why you're going to marry her? You make a good team? Like two mules yoked together and hauling hay?" She couldn't keep her disgust from showing through. "What an awful concept. Colt, have you turned into a social climber like my father?"

He set his cup down with a clatter. "Hal Glamorgan a social climber?" he questioned. "Where did you get a corkscrew idea like that?"

"I realized it a couple of years after my mother died."

There was a brief softening of his features. Colt had admired her mother. "How do you figure?"

"He wanted her to be on the board of charities and the opera and things like that. He wasn't satisfied with her as she was. Maybe he didn't mean to hurt her, but he did. She tried so hard to be what he wanted, but, Colt, she was a waitress in a small town when he met her. And he was a roustabout for an oil company.''

She fell silent, remembering that her mother had died coming home from a dinner for the board of directors of the symphony, to which she'd been appointed because of a large contribution from her father. Her mom, never a drinker, had drunk wine at the dinner. That was probably why she didn't notice the flash flood pouring through the creek on the way back to the ranch. She'd drowned when the car went under.

''Sometimes I wish you and Dad had never found that oil,'' she said, continuing. ''We used to be happy before we were rich. Before he wanted us to be something we weren't. That's the trouble with self-made men,'' she said slowly, the sadness overcoming her. ''They think they have the right to remake everyone else.''

''Belle—''

She stopped his lecture with a wave of her hand. ''Do you mind if I stay until morning? I'll clear out then, I promise.''

He rose and stood beside her, so close she felt his heat sweep over her in a sweet caress that filled her with poignant longing. He seemed pensive as he laid a hand on her shoulder. ''You can stay as long as you need to,'' he said huskily.

She gazed up at him and for a moment she saw something odd in his expression. His guard dropped. Emotion he'd never let her see flickered through his gaze. Then it was gone.

''As long as you behave and don't try to seduce

me again,'' he added with a sardonic smile, his mood changing.

A flush lit her face. ''I'm not a teenager anymore,'' she said with as much dignity as she could. ''I won't throw myself at you, so you needn't worry.''

He smiled. ''Ah, Belle, all grown-up, huh?''

She nearly melted at his feet when he used his old teasing manner with her. She hadn't known how much she'd missed it—and him—in her life.

He tugged on a strand of hair that fell over her shoulder. ''I'll miss that skinny tomboy who used to show me spiderwebs sparkling with dew and the speckled eggs in prairie hens' nests.''

Belle pulled away. ''She's gone. From now on, I'm going to be a hard-hearted businesswoman.'' At his skeptical snort, she added, ''I will be. That's why I'm here. I want you to teach me all I need to know. Will you?''

He was silent for so long she assumed he would say no. ''Maybe,'' he replied.

She frowned, sensing a condition in the word. ''Maybe?''

''If you'll do exactly what I tell you.''

''Of course.''

''There's no 'of course' about it. You'll give me your word to follow my orders exactly, or it's no deal.''

That was a no-brainer. She vowed to do precisely what he told her. ''You have my word.'' She crossed her arms and gave him a level stare, daring him to disbelieve her.

''All right. Monday we'll start. You have the weekend to prepare. Now go to bed.''

She resented his skeptical tone, but she didn't argue. Instead she nodded stiffly and headed for the bedroom. She went to sleep picturing herself as a femme fatale from an old television series—as sharp, sophisticated and hard-hearted as they come. That would be her model.

Colt would be so proud of her.

Colt took another sip of brandy, his eyes restlessly roaming the skyline as if some truth would suddenly appear and give him an insight into himself.

He'd been damn angry with Marsha tonight. A surprise, that. But then, so had her highfalutin attitude toward Belle. He hadn't liked that. It was one thing for him to be exasperated with her, but it was something else for an outsider to criticize her.

Belle was as close to family as he had. Her parents had taken him into their family circle as soon as they heard about the deaths of his parents. He'd been part of Hal's crew with a big oil company, a smart-aleck nineteen-year-old, swaggering to cover rejection by the love of his life, his high school sweetheart who had decided his prospects were too poor for her tastes. Lily, Belle's mother, had let him pour his heart out to her.

He swirled the brandy before taking another sip, then glared at the skyline again. Damn Hal and his will, his deathbed demand that Colt take care of Belle.

The tough tycoon had been afraid Belle would be taken in by some schemer out for her money, thus his plan to marry her off to someone of equal wealth, preferably a son of one of the early Texas families. Old money. Like Marsha.

Marsha was to the manor born. She came from true Texan stock, although he would never have known it from her clipped, cultivated accent. She sounded back East. She looked high-class. And he had the money to afford her.

For a second, he wondered at the cynicism inherent in this thought.

He was Texas born, too, as dirt-poor as the land his father had tried to ranch in the desert flats a hundred miles from El Paso. He wondered what his mother would have thought of Marsha.

He would never know. His parents had been killed in a tornado one dark night, their small frame house blown away as if it had never been. They hadn't lived to benefit from the wealth he'd made since striking oil eleven years ago in a wildcat operation with Harold Glamorgan.

With offshore finds that appeared to be bigger than the whole Alaska oil field, black gold was once again king in Texas. Did that make him a prince?

He snorted in wry amusement. He'd noticed that Marsha seldom spoke to anyone beneath her social level. A few years ago, she would have surely turned her nose up at him, too.

Maybe he was being too harsh. Most of the time she was as sweet as a pecan pie, a charming, sophisticated woman who viewed the world with a lofty disdain.

Not like Belle, who never met a stranger, who cried over lost pets no matter whom they belonged to and always had a moment to listen to other people's problems.

Belle.

Plan A—to turn Belle into a brilliant business-woman—hadn't worked so far. Her grades were high in all subjects…except finance, accounting and statistics courses, the core subjects she needed for a business career. She passed the courses, but it was evident she hated them.

Plan B—her father's idea to marry her off to a blue blood was the most practical one. *Old money, Colt. Belle can do better'n a couple of roustabouts like us, eh, lad?*

Colt sighed and leaned his head back on the sofa. A light scent, as familiar to him as the yellow sage that grew over much of Texas, hit his nose. He inhaled deeply.

Belle's scent. Pleasantly tart, sweet but hinting at herbs instead of flowers. He could remember being surrounded by it three years ago when she'd folded her slender body into his lap and declared she was ready for marriage and, oh, by the way, she wanted a half-dozen babies with him.

No coyness, no shyness, just the candid declaration she loved him and wanted him. He wondered what had flummoxed him more—her statement or his body's reaction to it, a reaction similar to the one he was experiencing now.

Funny how aware he'd been of Belle under him rather than Marsha on top of him as they struggled in a heap of arms and legs on the sofa.

A wave of heat blasted over him as if he'd stepped inside an oil-cracking tower. His hunger had shocked him three years ago. It still did. He wanted to take everything she offered—that bright eagerness for life, the sensual curiosity he wanted to satisfy—

He clamped down hard on his libido. One thing he wouldn't do was rob Belle of that sexy innocence. That was for her husband, some guy as young and in love with life as she was. She deserved that much.

When he'd had to reject her offer, he'd worried about hurting her, but she'd come through fine. No hothouse rose was Belle. She was a Texas bluebonnet, wild and hardy and tough to the tips of her roots. She was as stubborn as her dad and rarely took no for the final answer.

A smile pushed at the corners of his mouth in spite of his irritation. Now all he had to do was marry her off to one of the wealthy scions of an old Texas family. He'd made up a list of three names to concentrate on, with three other families that would be acceptable as backup. Belle would blow a gasket if she found out.

Hmm, Marsha might help. If he could convince her that helping with Belle might hasten the scamp out of his home. His instincts told him that was a bad idea. The two women mixed like tar and salt water. Marsha had made it clear if Belle was in his life she was out of it.

He tried to assess how that made him feel, but actually he felt sort of…nothing, not emptiness, not grief, not loneliness, nothing. Maybe he was incapable of feeling very deeply for anyone.

A memory intruded on his introspection. Belle, five years old and absolutely certain of her future. She'd climbed into his lap and snuggled against him. "I wuv you," she had announced to him and her parents. "I'm going to mawwy you. Is that okay?" she'd asked her mom.

Lily had smiled in her gentle way. "Of course. Colt is a wonderful choice—a gentleman in every way."

His chest tightened now as it had then. Lily had been teasing, but it had meant something to him to be accepted as part of their family.... That's what he missed most. It was the reason he was thinking of marriage.

Perhaps it was best his proposal had been interrupted earlier that evening. He'd turned thirty-four in May, less than a month ago. It had hit him that in another year he'd be thirty-five. Not exactly old, but still...

He figured it was time to marry and settle down. Marsha had seemed a good choice.

He'd been surprised when she'd grabbed his tie before he could turn on the light and guided him toward the twin black leather sofas. Women had been coming on to him since he made his first million, but Marsha had seemed so refined. He'd been almost afraid to kiss her the first time.

Tonight he'd planned to ask her to marry him, then turn out the lights, open the curtains to the view and make love to her.

He'd had to revise his schedule when she'd turned aggressive. So, okay, they would make love first, then he would ask her to marry him. The order hadn't been important. There was no reason to be a romantic about having everything perfect, including the presentation of the three-carat diamond nestled under the ivy on the coffee table.

Then Belle had screeched in his ear, disrupting all thoughts of romance in any form or order.

Finishing the brandy, he set the snifter aside and

snorted at Belle's idea. Teach her the business? Ha. He'd agreed to let her stay so he could marry her off.

Guilt nagged at him. Belle was an idealist. She believed in love and happily ever after. She'd hate being paraded before likely husband material like a prize filly at an auction.

But it was for the best. He would make sure the man had all the qualifications necessary to ensure Belle's happiness—wealth, integrity and gentleness. A man who would put Belle's welfare before his own, one who would be a tender husband to her and a caring father to their children. That's what he wanted for her.

He went to his study and made a list of likely candidates. He quelled any hitches of his conscience for interfering in her life with the harsh reminder of his promise to her father. He owed Hal for everything he had.

Yeah, it was best to get her married. Then she would have a husband to take over her business interests, and she could have her home and babies.

Then maybe *he* could have a life.

Chapter Two

Belle sang "The Yellow Rose of Texas" while she showered. She felt as buoyant as the first day of spring.

She considered her burst of happiness for a second, then shrugged. She saw no point in analyzing things to death. It was enough to be alive and in good health. Anything else was a gift.

Wrapping a towel around her wet hair and another around her body, she opened the bathroom door. Humming, she traipsed along the hall in her bare feet, feeling she could leap tall buildings in a single bound.

To prove it, she jumped into the air and clicked her heels together, a high school gymnastics feat she hadn't tried in years. Yep, she could still do it.

She grabbed the slipping towel and anchored it securely under her arms, tucking one end under the edge of the terry cloth to hold it in place.

At a sound behind her, she whirled around and met

the dark scowl of her host. She smiled brilliantly, determined not to notice his unfriendly countenance or the way her heart pounded erratically as he swept her with a frigid but thorough gaze.

"Colt, good morning." She peered at him more closely. "You look as if you slept in your clothes."

He was decidedly rumpled. A growth of beard shadowed his jaw, lending a sinister cast to his tanned face. A tuft of hair stuck up on the top of his head. It could have looked boyish and endearing...except Colt was never boyish, and *endearing* wasn't in his vocabulary.

A man who was bluntly honest, whose integrity a person could take to the bank, Colter McKinnon was the one person she trusted above all others.

"I did," he confessed, running a hand over his beard. "I fell asleep on the sofa."

She laughed. "You used to do that at our house. Mom would have me throw a blanket over you and leave you there. You did it on purpose so you could have some of her biscuits for breakfast." That gave her an idea. "I'll cook this morning. What would you like?"

"Don't bother," he ordered in chilling tones. "You'd better get dressed. We have a lot to do today."

Muffling her brightness in deference to his grouchy mood, she ducked into the guest room. After dressing in jeans and an orange T-shirt with a sequined cactus on the front, she tied her hair back and dashed for the kitchen.

As she passed Colt's door, she heard the shower running. Good. That should give her time.

She mixed up a batch of biscuits and stuck them in the oven while she fried sausage, then cooked four eggs. She put out jelly and set the table. Colt walked into the kitchen wearing a white shirt, a tie and dress pants just as she finished her tasks.

He frowned when the oven timer dinged and she removed the biscuits. She put them on a plate and wafted it under his nose.

"Surprise," she said, tossing a grin his way.

"This wasn't necessary," he told her, taking his seat, his body, rangy as a wild mustang, radiating tension.

He was really angry with her. It came as a shock, like believing the world was round, then seeing a picture from outer space showing it was square.

She took her chair. They ate in silence.

"I think," she began when they had finished, "I'd better find a job and an apartment."

His derisive snort indicated his opinion of that. "What are you qualified for?"

"Well, at boarding school they taught us which fork went with what course. I could get a job with a caterer setting up tables." She grinned.

"Can you type?"

"Of course. Hey, I've had computer classes. I could do data input."

"A minimum-wage job."

"An honest day's work," she countered. "I could wait tables. That's what Mom was doing when she met Dad."

"What have you learned at that fancy college?" He gave her a coolly assessing look.

She squirmed uneasily as if she were in an interview. "It's an all-female liberal arts school."

"Yeah?"

"Mmm, we studied the great religions of the world...and English. Literature. History."

"Didn't you take accounting and some business courses?"

Her face became warm. "Well, yes, but I...uh...sort of didn't learn much."

"Exactly."

She crossed her arms and glared at him. "You didn't go to college. Neither did my father."

"We learned in the hard-knocks school."

"Please, no 'walking to school barefoot in the snow' lectures. I've heard all the variations on that theme that could possibly exist."

"All right. We'll take it from the top and assume you didn't learn anything."

"That's a fair assessment." She gave him an impish grin. It didn't crack his disapproving facade for a minute.

"That T-shirt is atrocious."

Distracted, she looked down at the cheery color and sparkly cactus. "What's wrong with it?"

He ignored her and glanced at his watch. "I have a personal shopper scheduled for you at ten."

"A what?"

"Someone to help you with a business wardrobe. I'm not taking you to the office dressed like that."

"Today's Saturday," she protested.

"Haven't you heard time is money?"

"I hate money."

"You don't remember what it's like to live without it."

"I remember what it was like to be happy," she shot right back, feeling the black cloud of disapproval hovering over her head. Colt had once been her best friend.

But not since she'd thrown herself at him like a gawky kid with a crush on a hero. Never again. That was one lesson she wasn't likely to forget.

"Poor little you," he said with a mocking smile.

She firmed her lips and sat up straight. "Are you going to teach me the business or not?"

He stared at her so hard she broke into a sweat. Being on the hot seat exactly described the sensation.

"Yes. The first lesson is Dress For Success 101. Be ready to leave at nine forty-five." He poured a cup of coffee and went into his study, closing the door behind him.

Belle sighed in relief. Colt might not be willing, but he was a man of his word. He'd help her learn all she needed to know. Then she'd start her own business.

She tried to think what it might be, but nothing came to mind. She'd really like to live her days in the great outdoors and raise kids, horses and cattle. She'd been happy the few years they'd lived on a ranch. Before her mother died. Before her father decided he hated the place.

But life wasn't about being happy. It was time she learned to make her way in the cold, cruel world. She watched a few clouds drift over the flawless sky. Maybe, like Romeo and Juliet, she'd find her own niche.

Humming "A Place for Us," she went to dry her hair and prepare for her first lesson under Colt's tutelage.

"I saw the diamond."

Colt roused from his dark mood and flicked a glance at his guest. "What?"

"There was a jewelry box hidden under the ivy on the coffee table. I took a peek while I was waiting for you a few minutes ago. That's quite a rock. Marsha will love it, although she would probably prefer something bigger."

"That rock is three carats, kiddo."

"Yeah, like I said, Marsha would like something to match her barracuda smile."

"You met her once—and not in the best of circumstances—and you have her figured out?" He tossed her a sardonic glance that told her what he thought of her opinion.

Belle sighed loudly, clearly aggrieved at the injustice of his words. "I'm an excellent judge of character. Remember when Dad hired that foreman who turned out to be a crook?"

"Yeah, you diagnosed him as having beady eyes."

"He was part of a gang of rustlers. They would hire on at different ranches in an area, then steal hundreds of cattle. I was the one who followed him and found where they were stashing cows in that box canyon—"

Colt remembered the anger that had sizzled over him when she returned with her report, flushed with triumph and exhaustion after riding hell-for-leather for hours. She hadn't seemed to realize the danger she'd put herself in—a thirteen-year-old pitting herself against grown men. "That was a damn foolish thing to do," he reminded her.

A flush climbed into her cheeks. To his surprise, she didn't argue. Instead she studied him for a few seconds, then looked away.

It wasn't until they were in the car that she spoke again. "You forgot to take the ring so you'd have it at lunch today." She opened her shoulder bag and handed him the black velvet box.

He tossed it into the glove box.

"That's awfully expensive to leave lying around."

"I'll put it in the safe when I get to the office."

"You're not going to give it to her?"

"Not today."

"Good."

"Don't sound so relieved."

"You won't like being married to her." A frown etched two tiny lines above her nose.

No one had worried about him in years, not since Lily. It gave him a funny tingle in his chest. However, her certainty that he was making a mistake exasperated the hell out of him. "Have I asked you to be my marriage counselor?"

She grinned at him. He noticed the hint of dimple at each corner of her mouth. She had a sexy mouth—lush, ripe, ready for kissing games....

A jolt of awareness ran through him, shaking his composure. He whipped into a parking space and checked the time. Right on ten o'clock.

"The shopper's name is Kelley. You have money for lunch and a cab home when you're finished?"

"Yes."

"Show me."

She searched in her bag and pulled out two twenties. He nodded. She climbed out and headed for the door to the upscale department store. Watching her ramrod straight back and swinging stride, he experienced another surge of emotion that was gone so quickly he couldn't define it.

There was one thing he could detect without difficulty. His body was stiff and alert in a place it shouldn't be. A picture of her in her nightshirt, another in the towel that barely covered her rear, leapt into his mental vision.

He rubbed a hand over his face, shook his head, then managed a chuckle at his own predictable male reactions.

Belle was indeed growing up.

"Hello? Anybody here?" Belle stood in the middle of the small but elegant office and peered toward a door at the back. She wondered if she should knock on it.

"Just a minute."

She relaxed and chose one of the sturdier gilt chairs to sit on. She slouched down, crossed her ankles and yawned. After the long drive, then the late night, she was still tired this morning. Clothing was the farthest thing from her mind or interests. Besides, she didn't see anything wrong with jeans. They could have casual Friday every workday in her opinion.

Not that anyone ever asked what she wanted.

No, she wasn't going to be maudlin. Today was the first day of her new, hard-boiled persona. When the door opened, she pushed herself upright and crossed her legs at the knee.

Brown eyes, as large as a doe's, swept over her. The woman, Kelley Mosher by the nameplate on the desk, smiled a polite, professional smile and blinked several times. She was a small woman, shorter than Belle's five-seven height, with a delicate appearance. Her rich brown hair was swept into a neat do on top of her head.

"Hello, you must be Miss Glamorgan," she said in a soft contralto voice that reminded Belle of hot fudge sauce, warm and luscious.

"Belle, as in Starr. Are you Kelley?" The invisible vibration that emanates from a troubled person hit Belle as she stood to shake hands with the woman, who was in her late twenties, early thirties.

"Yes. Tell me about your wardrobe." Kelley's beautiful eyes swept over Belle's outfit.

"I must compliment you," Belle said with a laugh. "You managed to say that without a shudder." She tugged at her glittery T-shirt. "Salespeople have been known to faint when I walked into a shop."

Kelley laughed, too. "I see only an interesting challenge. Mr. McKinnon said you needed outfitting for work. An office position, I assume?"

"Sort of. I'm...a manager in training." That sounded pretty good.

The brown eyes widened slightly, but Kelley nodded solemnly. Over coffee they discussed a wardrobe.

Notebook and pen in hand, Kelley asked, "How many suits do you have? I need to know the material, weight and color."

"Mmm, well, actually, none."

"No suits? What about jackets?"

"I have a suede jacket, a ski parka and this really great black trench coat I got at a thrift shop. Oh, and a tweed coat with leather elbow patches."

"That's it?"

Belle screwed up her face and thought. "Yeah. Well, a couple of nylon jogging jackets."

"Ensembles such as dresses with a wrap?"

"Nope."

"Skirts?"

"Oh, yes. Two for square dancing with heaps of crinoline. I haven't worn them in three or four years, though. And a denim skirt for going out to dinner." Belle noted a gleam of desperation appearing in the liquid brown eyes. She added, "I have a cocktail outfit. Black pants with a black shell and an overblouse in black with gold threads in it."

"Shoes?"

"I wear sandals or sneakers most of the time. I have a pair of nice dress boots," she offered helpfully as Kelley bit her lip and looked despondent.

"To wear with the denim skirt for going out to dinner?"

Belle beamed. "Right."

"Miss Glamorgan—"

"Belle."

"Belle." Kelley clicked her pen nervously. "I don't mean to hurt your feelings…"

"That's okay. No one else minds in the least." She thought of Colt and his icy girlfriend.

"You might need an entire wardrobe."

"I know. I've accepted I can't wear this outfit to the office. Colt made that pretty clear."

"The jeans with the tweed jacket and a tailored shirt would be fine for casual Friday, maybe with a colorful scarf around your throat."

"Scarves always remind me of old men trying to look younger than their years."

Kelley studied her in total silence for a long minute. "Would you mind standing up?"

Belle jumped to her feet.

Kelley walked all around her. "You are close to runway perfect."

"No figure, you mean?" Belle wrinkled her nose and surveyed her form in the full-length mirrors. "I'm not as skinny as I was a couple of years ago."

"You're not skinny. You have a long, angular bone structure. You'll be able to carry a lot of weight before you look even mildly plump."

"Thanks. I think."

"Clear jewel tones—ruby, emerald, amber. We'll get you into a suit with a couple of skirts to get you started. A solid skirt with your tweed jacket would work, too. There's a dress I know will be perfect." She went to her desk and picked up the telephone.

In a few minutes, clerks began to arrive, each carrying items of clothing. Belle began to enjoy herself. After all, she was female....

Her arms were full of parcels when she arrived home. The doorman helped her into the elevator. "Thank you, Mr. Cheaver," she said as he stuck the card in the slot that allowed her to go to Colt's penthouse. "How's your daughter?" she remembered to ask.

Four years ago, the doorman had confided his daughter wasn't doing well in school. The counselor had thought the girl wasn't bright enough to finish school. Belle had appealed to Colt, who had arranged testing, then special tutoring when they'd found the girl was dyslexic.

The deep lines in his face creased slightly upward. "Fine. Dee graduated from high school and got a job in a bank. She's also taking extra accounting courses."

"That's great."

Mr. Cleaver pushed the button for the top floor, then stepped off the elevator. "She doesn't like her boss. She wants to start her own business. I don't know where she gets her ideas." Shaking his head, he returned to his post near the front door of the ten-story building.

Belle smiled, but her sympathy was for the girl. Boys were encouraged to be independent, but females had no such luck. The elevator door slid closed. Belle was whisked to the penthouse. She could hardly wait to show Colt her new look. Kelley had helped her find the blend of sophisticated and casual outfits that personally suited her.

"Belle?" Colt pushed the door closed with his shoulder. He carried a bag of Chinese takeout in each hand.

"Coming. Close your eyes."

He huffed under his breath and headed for the kitchen. Without closing his eyes, he spread the food on the table and set the plates and forks out. He made a pot of green tea he knew Belle liked and opened a bottle of blush wine.

"Are your eyes closed?" she demanded, sticking her head around the door frame.

He rolled his eyes toward the ceiling, then indulged her playful antics. "Okay, they're closed."

"Ta-dum. Okay, you can look now."

He did a double take. A stranger in a ruby dress stood in front of him. The material draped in a soft crisscross over her breasts. A black belt cinched it in at her tiny waist, bringing attention to a slender torso and perfect shape. Modest gold earrings nestled against her earlobes and a simple chain adorned her neck. With black pumps and purse, her hair cut short in front and feathered back over her ears, but still long in back, she looked ready for a photo shoot.

"Watch this."

She slipped out of sight, then reappeared. The pumps were gone, replaced with black tasseled loafers. A tweed jacket of black, gray and amber with subtle red and blue threads and black leather patches, covered the dress. She looked ready for a weekend at a country manor.

"I brought supper," he said, unable to think of another thing to say.

"Okay. I'll show you the rest after we eat. Kelley was great." Belle's voice faded as she returned to her room. In a minute, she bounced into the kitchen in gray sweats.

Colt helped himself to food from the white cartons and pushed them across the table to her. Belle looked her normal self. For a moment there, she'd been someone he didn't know, the girl next door who had left home and returned a fashion model or something. It had almost unnerved him.

He hadn't realized her waist was so slender. And she'd filled out nicely up top, too. He'd have no trouble marrying her off.

"So you liked Kelley?" he asked.

"Yes. She was wonderful. Isn't it terrible about her folks feuding with the neighbors, though?"

"I didn't know they were." He split a pair of wooden chopsticks and expertly picked up a piece of browned meat and stuck it in his mouth.

"She told me a little about it over lunch. I think there's more to the story, though. How did you meet her?"

"I haven't. Marsha suggested her. She's used her before and thought she might be good for you."

Belle wrinkled her nose.

"No doubt you wouldn't have liked her if you'd known Marsha recommended her," he mentioned dryly. "I'd never have taken you for a narrow-minded person, Belle, or someone to make snap judgments."

"Do you still have the ring?"

He frowned in annoyance as she totally ignored his statement and brought up the ring. "Yes."

She sighed in relief. "Marsha is a barracuda. She's after your money."

"That's ridiculous. Her father is one of the movers and shakers of Texas. He went to college with the governor."

"Big deal. I say she's looking for the main chance. Want to put a dollar where your mouth is?"

He scowled at her.

"Afraid I'm right? I am an excellent judge of character, you know."

"Yes. You've mentioned it frequently over the

years. You're wrong in this case." He grinned. "Jealous, Belle?"

"Yes. If you won't take me, I'd at least like to see you with a decent person."

He choked on a bite of sweet-and-sour pork, then muttered an expletive picked up from his days in the oil fields. She grinned unrepentantly.

"You're a menace," he told her.

"You, too. You've had your hair cut since you stopped by school at Easter. Very stylish, although I liked the wild and dangerous look."

"Marsha thought it unkempt. She didn't like it hanging over my collar."

"Yeah, sounds like her."

"You need to get over this childish prejudice," he taunted. "You could learn a thing or two from her."

"Didn't I floor you with my sophisticated look? You could hardly take your eyes off that red number."

Colt felt the flush hit him midchest and climb up his neck. "Spoken like a true lady," he chided grimly, aware of exactly what she'd looked like in the red outfit.

"Do I have to be a lady with you?" she asked on an oddly wistful note. She propped her foot on the chair and peered at him over her knee while she scooped rice out of the carton with the set of chopsticks.

He got a mental image of her leap into the air, the silent click of her heels, the bath towel slipping down her back.... He thought of those from-here-to-forever legs of hers wrapped around him. Sweat broke out on his upper lip.

"Yes. A lady is always a lady." He jabbed a piece of pork, then plopped it in his mouth and chewed angrily.

She nodded. "I have a problem, an ethical one. Do you think it's all right that I charged my new clothes? The bill goes to the trust account. I didn't have enough money to pay for them myself. Although I got the bare minimum Kelley said I would need to get me started," she assured him.

Colt considered. "You have a clothing allowance."

"That's only if I stay in school."

"I'll okay the expense. You can repay the account when you draw your salary."

"That may be years from now."

"The company will pay you for your work when you start Monday. You'll be paid the following week. Do you need an advance?"

"I'll be paid real money? For learning the business?"

Her mouth turned upward. Her eyes glowed like dark amber. The concept of a salary was obviously foreign to her.

He was glad he'd thought of it. Belle had lived on an allowance all her life, having to account for every cent she spent, per Hal's instructions. Her father had wanted her to be cost-conscious. Those strictures would disappear when she came of age.

Colt watched her sample the food in one of the boxes. Maybe he could move things along. One of the young men on the list lived on a ranch next to one he'd bought a couple of months ago, a present to himself so he could get out of the city more often.

He'd throw a party or something and introduce the young people.

Then all he'd have to do was let nature take its course. He frowned. The rich kid better make sure he had a wedding ring on Belle's finger before getting too chummy, or else he'd have Colter McKinnon to answer to.

Colt relaxed. He had broken up more than one fight among the roustabouts in the oil fields. He could handle any punk who didn't treat Belle right.

Chapter Three

Belle stretched her back wearily. She brushed the dust off the rear of her skirt.

"Ready?" Colt asked, sticking his head around the storage room doorway.

"Yes." She yawned, closed the file cabinet and trotted along after his retreating form like a trained retriever. She'd been relegated to filing closed records and to tossing those over seven years old in the recycling bin.

At first she'd been resentful of her lowly job, then she'd grown interested as she started reading the reports and correspondence. During one short week, she'd learned that her father had mostly played poker with his cronies while Colt took care of their business interests.

When she'd mentioned this to Colt last night, he'd cautioned her about believing the obvious. Her father had taught him all he knew of the oil business.

"What about the stock investments and the pipe-line supply business that you bought?" she had demanded.

"What else was there to do with the money?" he'd asked laconically.

She thought of all the things he could have wasted money on—like a six-carat diamond for the barracuda. She stopped by the ladies' room and washed the grime from her hands. She hadn't realized filing was such dusty work.

No one had even seen her outfit. She wore a skirt of red, gray and amber plaid with a red cotton sweater. Kelley had said red was her best color. The charcoal gray shoes were made like loafers, but with one-inch heels to make them a bit dressier.

When she joined Colt in his office, he was ready to go. Her heart lumped in her throat as she stood beside him in the elevator of the huge office building where Gulfco Enterprises had its own floor. She'd learned Gulfco was now a holding company because it held the shares of the other companies they owned, each of which operated as a separate company. Colt acted as overseer of all their operations.

She was intensely aware of him, as if her skin became sensitized in his presence. He was dressed casually in tan cords, a dark blue shirt that did mysterious things to his gray eyes and a tweed sports jacket.

There was a part of her that wanted to lean into him, to slide into his warmth and cling like soft candle wax, their bodies mingled in the most intimate way. Another part wanted to be independent of him, to stand on her own and not need him as a safety net.

"I think I'd better try to find a place to live," she

finally said when the silence became too much. "With my paycheck—thank you very much—and the money I'll save in tuition costs, I can afford a place of my own. Maybe I can look around this weekend."

"I thought we'd go to the ranch. I'm having a dinner tomorrow night."

"There is no..." Her voice wobbled. She swallowed hard to hold the ridiculous tears in.

"Not your old place. I bought my own spread near here. I'm having some neighbors over to break the ice. I thought you might like to meet them. Of course, if you're too busy..." He let the words trail off.

"Of course not," she said, and immediately wondered at the smile that barely touched the corners of his mouth. She got the feeling she'd been manipulated. But that was okay. Wild horses couldn't keep her away from his place.

"You really have a ranch?"

"Yeah. A kingdom of my very own."

"How big?"

"It's only five hundred acres, maybe two hundred cows."

"Does it have a house?"

"Yes. The old ranch house burned, and the owners built a new one about four years ago."

"I hope they put on a tin roof. They sound wonderful when it rains, especially at night when you're lying all snug in bed and listening to it. I love that."

"Yes, it has a tin roof." He gave her a narrow-eyed scrutiny, then looked away, his expression closed.

Her mind went off on tangents of its own, envisioning horses and kids and herself...and Colt?

Not him. Not for her.

She pulled herself from the dangerous place where childish dreams banged into harsh reality. She'd learned a lesson three years ago. Colt didn't want her in his life.

At his penthouse, she changed to jeans and boots and a red T-shirt with Snow White and the dwarfs prancing on front in glittery white flocking. When Colt stopped at her door, she was dithering over what to take with her.

"The red number for dinner tomorrow night," he suggested. "Jeans for the rest of the time. Bring a jacket. I thought we might go riding."

"Great." She quickly packed a weekend case. "Ready."

He drove southwest of Dallas for nearly an hour before leaving the highway for a county road. In fifteen minutes, he turned onto a paved drive. Five minutes after that, he pulled into a three-car garage attached to a two-story ranch house of brick and stucco.

"Very nice," she commented.

He grunted something that could have been a reply or a growl and led the way inside. The family room and a large dining room flowed into the kitchen, the dividing walls from four to eight feet in height rather than going all the way to the fourteen-foot ceilings. The feeling was one of openness and comfort. A fireplace of fieldstone dominated the family room.

There was also a living room, den and master suite downstairs. Colt put her in one of three bedrooms upstairs, each complete with a gorgeous vista. Her room was decorated in poppy gold with brilliant red touches and had an alcove with two chairs and a table.

"I love it," she told him, rushing to the window to check the view. She knelt on the padded seat.

A bluff of limestone glistened in the sun. A creek ran at its base. Stock tanks and barbed wire fences delineated fields of grazing Herefords. The house sat on a small rise overlooking it all.

When she turned back to the room, the doorway was empty. Her smile faded.

She settled back on the window seat and gazed at the broad vista visible from her elevated perch. The sky was darkening into deep twilight, streaked with magenta, purple and blue tones.

Her heart stirred restlessly. She was haunted by the things that might have been but would never be.

How foolish it was to dream.

The return of grief tugged at her like an insistent child demanding attention. When her mother died, her father had sent her to a boarding school in Virginia. There she'd learned to sit an English saddle, to ride to hounds in an imaginary fox chase—they laid down a scent trail, but no real fox was involved—and to serve an afternoon tea.

But the loneliness, ah, yes, the loneliness. After a week, she'd made plans to run away.

Colt had saved her. He'd called her each and every Sunday morning. He'd surprised her with visits each semester. He'd sent her a wreath of yellow sage to hang on her door. She'd loved him more than anything.

Propping her arms on her knees, she contemplated her future. Nothing came to mind. Where once she'd felt as if she'd burst with life and ideas, now there was only a determination to see it through, to get from one day to the next because she had to.

"Ready to eat?" Colt called up the steps.

Belle roused from her musing, the strange loneliness congealing to an ache deep inside. She'd experienced it before. She only needed to wait it out and the pain would gradually fade. "Coming."

They joined his foreman, Matt Taylor, Matt's wife, Ginny, and their four sons, aged eleven to seventeen, for a dinner of grilled steak, barbecued beans and fried potatoes. The steak was cooked Texas-style— black on the outside and done in the middle.

"Can you ride?" Jason, the youngest of the Taylor boys, wanted to know.

"Yes."

"You want to go to the cascades tomorrow?" He quickly checked his father to see how the older man took this. The foreman smiled and didn't object.

Belle looked a question at Colt. She didn't know what their schedule was.

"As long as you can play hostess tomorrow night," he said in a sardonic tone.

"Sounds fun," she told Jason. They smiled at each other like conspirators.

"I'll ride along," the oldest son, John, put in.

"You got that section of fencing to check," Matt told him. "You get that done, then you can think about squiring the girls around."

John's ears turned red. Belle saw the middle two boys grin at the oldest brother's discomfort. She cut into her steak. "This is delicious. It's been a coon's age since I've had steak and real Texas fries."

After the meal she helped Mrs. Taylor with the dishes, then returned to the ranch house. Colt had disappeared with his foreman to go over the coming spring schedule. She watched television in the family room after changing to a nightshirt and robe. At eleven she went to bed. Colt still hadn't come in when she finally went to sleep.

"Let's run 'em," Jason shouted, and dashed ahead on his pinto.

Picking up his spirit of fun, she nudged her mustang into a canter. Soon they were in an all-out run across the wide meadow. Cows scattered in front of them while those to the side looked on with a wary alertness.

The sun was bright, the air brisk. As always, when she was in the great outdoors, her spirits revived and she felt she could conquer the world. How did people stand to be cooped up in offices all their lives? No wonder the world was full of crazies.

"Race you to that oak tree growing out of the ledge," Jason challenged when she and her mount came alongside.

"You're on. I'll count to three. One. Two. Three." Laughing, she took off, Jason hot on her heels.

She pulled back a little so that they passed the oak in a dead heat. They pulled up at the creek and dismounted, leaving the horses ground hitched.

The horses sucked the water noisily. Belle took a drink from Jason's canteen. They explored farther up the creek, which tumbled over limestone boulders as big as cars.

"There's a cave," Jason told her, pointing across the cascade.

"Show me."

She followed him, leaping from boulder to boulder over the frothing white water to the other side.

From a distance, Colt watched the two scramble over the boulders like young mountain goats on a romp. Belle didn't hesitate at any spot, but jumped right across, following Jason's lead. The eleven-year-old was clearly smitten with her.

Across the way, they ducked their heads and peered into the shallow depression of a cave which tapered to a crack about ten feet into the limestone crevice. Jason had brought Colt there on his first visit to the ranch.

He watched while the youngster and Belle straddled boulders and removed their shoes and socks. They were going to wade in the spring-fed creek.

Shaking his head at their howls of agony and laughter upon sticking their feet into the cold water, he rode the big, bony gelding past the oak growing out of a shelf of rock and stopped beside the creek.

"Yo, Jason," he called. "Your mom says your friend Timothy called. You're invited to spend the night at his house and go to a movie. Interested?"

"Yes, sir!"

"Take off. Your mom will drop you in town when she goes in to get the groceries."

Jason grabbed his shoes, then glanced at Belle.

"I'll see that she doesn't get lost on her way back," he called to reassure the lad.

In less than five minutes, Jason was on his way.

Colt watched Belle who continued to sit on the

boulder, her feet warming in the sun. He dropped his reins and used the boulders for stepping stones until he joined her.

"You look happier than I've seen you all week," he said, straddling the rock Jason had vacated.

"I like it here. You're really lucky to find a place this close in. You can come out every weekend." She smiled at him. "I'd commute to the ranch every night."

An odd sensation stole over him. Studying her face, it was like looking at Belle and yet it wasn't. The shadows of a pine cast indentations under her cheekbones. Mysteries slumbered in her eyes. He knew her, and yet he didn't.

This wasn't Belle, the child who had wept on his shoulder in loneliness and despair when her parents died. Yet something of that girl lingered in the wistful line of those lush, kiss-inviting lips, in the tremulous set of this young woman's mouth.

He sensed she hadn't taken that final step into womanhood, but she was poised and ready for it, to share her body, to give of herself and her dreams, to take another into her deepest confidences. Belle, he realized, was ready to fall in love.

Need, harsh and demanding, broke over him. All he had to do was reach out and take...

"We'd better start back," she said, her voice almost foreign to him in its new maturity and womanly awareness.

The air rushed in a breathless hush that blew softly over his face. It ruffled the feathery wisps of hair at her temples and over her ears. He brushed them off her cheeks and stayed to caress the warmth of her skin.

Her eyes flicked to his and opened wider, as if startled by what she saw. She became very still.

He trailed his fingers to her lips. They were moist, tender, delectable. He should move away. He didn't. Instead he bent forward and brushed across them experimentally. They were as soft as they looked, bare of lipstick, yet luscious.

"Sweet," he heard himself say, his tone low, dropping to the husky register that preceded sex. He dragged air into his lungs and inhaled the fragrance of sage and Belle's own spicy sweet scent. A mighty wind rushed through his head, drowning out all sense.

There was only the moment and the radiance of the sun and the need, the surprising need...

His horse snorted and whickered into the wind. Colt jerked back just before his mouth crashed down on Belle's in a kiss both of them would regret.

"Let's go."

He saw confusion, then disappointment sweep through her eyes. She was young Belle, after all. He could still read her emotions. She blinked and the brief revelation was gone.

"Yes," she agreed, pulling on socks and boots, "we need to get ready for your guests."

He mentioned his neighbor's son was home from school for the weekend with another friend. When he said the names, she grimaced.

"Todd and Gary are two of the Neanderthals from the university. They used to come to dances at my college. I can't stand them. But I'll be nice," she assured him when he cast a startled glance her way.

"Well, I guess I can cross those two off," he murmured, mentally removing the first two names on his list of likely mates for Belle. He ignored the sense of relief her dislike produced.

"You can't uninvite them." She clicked her feisty mare into a faster pace to keep up with the gelding.

"Right. We just won't have them over again."

"Good."

He smiled at the satisfaction in her tone. One thing about Belle—a person would always know where he stood with her. She hadn't an ounce of subterfuge in her body.

"Don't tell them," Belle advised.

'That I'm seeing Jamie?" Kelley looked worried.

"You're thirty years old. You can date whoever you want to. It's no business of your parents."

"They hate his family."

"The lawsuit over that piece of land was in your grandparents' day, for heaven's sake. Besides, when they see how happy you are, they'll be happy for you. And probably relieved that you aren't going to be an old maid."

"I've tried to forget him, but when we ran into each other that day at the cleaners, it was like…like we'd never been apart. We just started talking and talked until two in the morning."

Belle thought the story wonderfully romantic. Kelley and Jamie had been college sweethearts who had broken up because of their parents' animosity. Now they'd met again after he was transferred to Dallas by his company.

"You should elope," she told Kelley.

"My mother would never forgive me. She wants me to wear my grandmother's wedding dress."

"Well, then, you just have to take a firm stand. Tell your folks you've met the most wonderful guy and you want to marry—wait! I got it. Tell them you're pregnant."

Kelley nearly spewed her tea across the table. "Give a signal when you're going to lob a grenade at me," she requested, patting her mouth on the pink linen napkin.

"No, really. You know how stuffy parents are. They'll be so thrilled that you're going to marry and be respectable that they'll throw themselves on Jamie's neck in gratitude."

The idea was so ridiculous, they both laughed.

"It's your life," Belle said on a quieter note. "You can't live it to please them."

"The way you've tried to please Colt by going to schools and taking courses you hated?"

Belle sighed. "That's different. I mean, it's just school, not my life. Maybe you two should live together."

"We're thinking the same thing. Jamie's mom died last year, but his dad is as ornery as mine." She looked at her watch and stood. "Well, back to work. That outfit looks lovely on you."

Belle was wearing the royal blue suit Kelley had chosen along with a pale pink silk blouse. "Thanks. My personal shopper has excellent taste. I recommend her."

Still smiling, Belle dashed along the lunch-hour sidewalk traffic and returned to the office. She couldn't figure out what the forty people did who worked for Colt and the holding company. There were accountants, and payroll processing for all the other companies, a computer department and buyers who scouted out good deals for everything from heavy equipment for the pipeline business to toilet tissue for everyone.

She relieved Colt's secretary at the front desk. The receptionist was out with the flu, so Belle had gotten promoted from file clerk to telephone answerer, letter opener and coffee maker.

Colt returned shortly after she had settled in. She wondered if he'd had lunch with the delectable Marsha and ignored the hot ripple of jealousy that ran through her. She tried not to notice how the very air seemed to vibrate when he walked in.

"Hi. Did you have a nice lunch?"

He gave her a calculating glance, then nodded. He'd been silent and wary around her since that odd moment by the creek when she'd thought he was going to kiss her, *really* kiss her. Of course he hadn't, but she'd wanted it.

"I'm having some people over Friday night," he said. "Order whatever food we need for about twenty people."

She covered her surprise and grabbed a memo pad. "A buffet dinner or hors d'oeuvres?"

"Hors d'oeuvres, but heavy."

"Got it." She wrote a note in the margin of the memo.

Colt sat on the corner of her desk. "Walters is someone I'm courting. I want to buy one of his companies. He likes American primitive art and pioneer artifacts."

"Okay, I'll discuss Grandma Moses with him."
She grinned when Colt frowned at her tone. "And I'll
be nice. Wasn't I impressive with the Neanderthals?
Didn't I wow them with my wide-eyed wonder at
their corny stories?"

"You bowled them over in that red dress. They
were practically fighting over who got to do the most
for you. They were fetching and carrying as if they
were two dogs chasing a stick."

"I told you they were dumb."

"Dumb-struck. Where did you learn those little
tricks with the eyes and the lips?"

Her smile faltered. Colt had always been her champion. It hurt to know she displeased him. And yet she
couldn't figure out exactly what she was doing wrong
in his eyes.

"A woman knows womanly things," she countered.

He was suddenly closer, his lips thin with anger.
"Just how much of a woman are you?"

"I—I don't know." What was he talking about?

He stood and strode away, then stopped at the window to stare down at the traffic ten stories below. He
jammed his hands in his pockets and kept his back to
her.

She rose and went to him. Laying her hand on his
shoulder, she leaned against his arm. "Do you want
me to leave, Colt? I've interfered in your life enough.
You'd probably be engaged and happy by now if it
weren't for me."

"No, I don't want you to leave," he muttered savagely. He whirled on her and pulled her close with

his hands on her shoulders. "But it's damned hard, Belle."

"What is?" She stared up at him anxiously.

He gave a snort of laughter. "The situation."

She suddenly understood. "Oh, I see. You miss...you were probably used to having Marsha over..." She forced the words out. "If you want to stay at her place sometime, that's okay. I don't mind staying alone."

His fingers tightened painfully, then relaxed. He laughed out loud, a harsh sound that didn't indicate humor.

"How can you be so incredibly naive?" he asked. "I haven't slept with Marsha. That isn't the problem."

"Well, what is it?"

"Me. And the fact that I want to take you home and do all kinds of things that would probably horrify your virgin sensibilities."

She felt as if a ton of snow had been dumped on her. The sensation immediately turned from cold to hot, as if lava bubbled through her blood. She couldn't think of a thing Colt might want to do to her that would horrify her at all. She was ready to learn whatever he wanted to teach.

"Like what? Show me," she demanded.

He drew a breath through clamped teeth. "No."

"Kiss me."

"Absolutely not." He gave her a little shake.

"I'm dizzy," she whispered, "just thinking of it."

She was. The idea of Colt doing sexy things to her was endlessly fascinating. Her mind spun like a whirl-wind out of control. She closed her eyes and swayed toward him, mindless of the perils his caress might bring.

"Quit acting like a love-struck kid," he ordered in a gritty voice. "We've been through this already."

Setting her away from him, he strode into his office and closed the door with a decisive slam meant to shut her out. She put her hands to her flaming cheeks as humiliation washed over her. Hadn't she learned anything in three years?

But it wasn't all her this time. Colt was involved, too, although he didn't want to be. There was something, an attraction, between them.

She sat down before her knees collapsed and tried to sort it out. Every nerve in her body jumped when Colt yanked open the private door into his office.

"Don't read anything into what I said," he advised. "I'm a man. I react to curious virgins like any other. Don't get any ideas."

"Maybe I'm not the one with ideas," she informed him. "Maybe it's your own ideas that are bothering you."

He took one menacing step into the room, then stopped. This time when he laughed it was real. "You got that right, kiddo." Still chuckling, albeit with a wry twist to his mouth, he closed the door and retreated.

Belle shook her head. And men complained that women were hard to understand!

Chapter Four

Belle sampled a lobster roll, then a thin slice of pâté. "Delicious." She licked her fingers as she went to check the living room. "Very nice," she told the caterer, an older man with a mustache and a French accent.

He stepped back and surveyed the flowers on the coffee table. He'd wanted to bring in elaborate bouquets in tall baskets for each side of the French doors leading to the balcony, but she had vetoed the idea. Colt had given her a budget, and she'd stuck to it...no matter how tempting the flambé station had sounded.

She caught sight of herself in the huge panels of glass next to the balcony doors. She wore her cocktail outfit—black toreador pants, a slinky top and a black over-jacket with gold threads. Maybe black made her look too thin.

"You look charming," the caterer said.

Embarrassed at being caught staring at her own image, she flicked imaginary lint from her jacket. "Thank you, Monsieur Pierre. The pâté loaf is the best I've ever tasted. I know everyone will be wild over it. Do you give out your recipes, should anyone ask?"

"*Mais oui,*" he assured her. "But, of course."

She drifted around the penthouse, waiting for Colt to vacate his study. She wanted his approval before their first guests arrived. His near-fiancée wasn't on the guest list she'd seen, but he might have invited Marsha personally rather having Carmen Blue, his secretary, call her.

Belle wanted everything to be perfect, but not because of the socialite. She wanted everyone, including Colt, to see that she, too, could be the perfect hostess.

"Did you check the liquor cabinet? Henry likes a Scotch after dinner. I thought I had an unblended one."

Colt crossed the carpet and sorted through the liquor cabinet, part of a black lacquer-and-glass wall unit built for that purpose. Looking at him, she acknowledged the pulse of excitement that flowed through her. He was incredibly handsome in a black evening suit with a white shirt and black silk tie. A red-and-black silk handkerchief added the only splash of color.

Mysterious. Dangerous. Enchanting.

The descriptive words floated through her mind as she hurried forward. "No, I didn't think about liquor, other than three wines to go with the food."

"Ah, here it is. Aged twenty years, single malt. This is the one." He took the crystal container to his study and returned to the middle of the living room.

"Henry and I will have our meeting in there. Think you can keep everyone else entertained while we talk?"

"Sure."

He grinned, stunning her with the complexity of it, the beauty, the irony, the hidden nuances she sensed but couldn't name. "Belle, the confident hostess."

She shrugged with studied insouciance. "I've done it often enough for my father. If you didn't think I could handle it, you should have called in Marsha."

"Oh, I knew you could handle it."

His attitude bothered her. It had all week. He seemed to have become harder, more cynical of life, amused by her attempts to learn the business.

"What does Mr. Walters have that you want?"

"A supply business that fits our needs. Drill heads mostly, and mud."

Mud was what oil men called the slurry used in drilling. When her father had taken her to the wells with him, they both came home covered in it. Her mother would scold, then laugh....

"What is it? What's troubling you?" Colt stood in front of her, a frown converging into a line between his thick, dark eyebrows.

"Nothing. I was thinking of... Nothing."

"The early days," he said quietly, "when Lily was alive and you were happy."

She searched his eyes, but couldn't detect any mockery in them. "Yes."

"Is your life so awful now?"

"Not really. It's just that it's hard to be adrift, to have no one." She stopped, realizing that Colt had no family, either. He'd been an orphan for years.

He hooked a finger under her chin and studied her face. "Haven't I always been here when you needed a shoulder to cry on?"

"Yes, but—"

"But?"

She moved away from his touch and pulled up a smile. "I don't need a shoulder anymore. I only cry at sad movies and sentimental TV commercials nowadays."

The doorbell rang.

"Our guests," he said. He took her hand and tucked it into his arm. "Let's invite them in."

To Belle's relief, she didn't have to face his girlfriend that night. The twenty guests were all businesspeople. She'd talked to several of them the past week while she filled in for the receptionist. She recalled Mr. Walters as soon as she heard his voice.

He spoke in a bass tone which went with his massive size. His attitude was typically Texan, expansive and confident. His son Slocum was as tall, but hadn't filled out with his father's bulk. He had the deep voice, but was quieter in manner and speaking. His blue eyes and sun-streaked blond hair were very attractive. She judged him to be about twenty-eight.

"Glamorgan," Henry repeated. "Any kin to Harold Glamorgan?"

"My father," she admitted.

"Meanest poker player I ever met," Henry told her. It was a compliment. "Sorry to hear it when he died."

"Thank you." She turned to the son. "Do you live in the city or are you a rancher?"

"I'm the son with the law degree."

She accepted a glass of wine and selected a slice of pâté from the tray the waiter held for them. Slocum opted for the liquor cabinet and a brandy.

"So there are other sons? What are their degrees?"

Slocum grimaced. "One older brother. He has the MBA."

She knew at once Slocum was unhappy in his life. They drifted over to the windows and watched the city in silence for a moment. "What would you rather be?"

He roused from his introspection. "Oh, I like law well enough. A lot, actually. It's my father that's driving me up the wall."

"I know exactly what you mean. My father had this idea I should be a tycoon. Colt is teaching me the business."

Slocum looked impressed. "Dad thinks McKinnon is a man on the rise. He told my brother to study his moves."

Belle found she liked Slocum more than any young man she'd ever known. "What's the problem between you and your father?"

"He disapproves of the woman I want to marry."

Belle was at once sympathetic. "Do you love her very much? Does she love you?"

He hesitated, then nodded. "Mary is wonderful. She's a nurse. When I fell off a horse and broke my collarbone, some friends took me to an emergency-care clinic. That's how we met. It was...well..."

"Love at first sight?"

His ears turned red. "Yeah. She's a wonderful person, but my father has decided she's after my money. Money, ha! He's got the purse strings tighter than...well, pretty tight. My brother and I work for a pittance.''

"No one should be a slave to relatives. Why don't you get another job?''

"My mom. She has a weak heart. She can't stand for the family to quarrel.'' His sigh was despondent.

Belle laid a sympathetic hand on his sleeve. "That's too bad, but surely your mother wants you to be happy. You mustn't let your father stand in the way.''

"Mary agrees with my father.''

"That she's a gold digger?'' Belle exclaimed, horrified.

"No. That she wouldn't be right for me. It's just that she's older than I am. She thinks I would regret marrying her, that I'll meet someone younger—''

He broke off and stared at Belle until she felt uneasy.

"What is it?'' she asked.

"I don't suppose you would...no, never mind.''

"What?'' Belle helped herself to another glass of wine.

"My father likes you,'' he said slowly. "If he thought I was seeing you, then maybe I'd have time to convince Mary to give us a chance...forget it.''

Belle thought it a very romantic plan. "That's a wonderful idea. Listen, we could double-date, only we'd pretend that you and I were together.''

"Assuming I could talk Mary into playing along, who would we get for her?''

Belle frowned thoughtfully. She looked across the room. Colt and Mr. Walters were just coming out of the study. Colt gave her a severe frown. She smiled brilliantly at Slocum. "I know just the person."

Colt wondered how he'd let himself be talked into this. He hated opera. Except for a few passages, it all sounded like screeching to him. Slocum Walters had tickets for a charity benefit by three tenors.

Belle had assured him this would be a riveting performance. He hoped so. He hadn't slept well that week. Maybe because Belle had been out with or had the Walters kid over every blasted night.

Not that he had anything against Slocum, other than he was a lawyer. An unfair assessment, he knew, but there it was. He was irritated at his own feelings.

Belle took Slocum's calls in her bedroom as if they shared a secret. That, too, irritated the hell out of Colt. There was something very suspicious going on.

Colt glanced past the woman beside him to Slocum, then on to Belle, sitting on the far side. Slocum paid more attention to Mary Cline, who was supposed to be *his* date, than to Belle, who was with the lawyer.

Belle leaned forward and grinned at him when she saw him watching her. She was wearing black slacks with a red sweater set. The pearls at her throat and ears were from him for her seventeenth birthday. Which she'd spent alone at the fancy boarding school.

Hal had been involved in a big poker tournament and had forgotten the event. So he had flown up to see her and take her out to dinner to celebrate. That had been a mistake. It was probably when she developed her crush on him and assumed they would marry when she graduated.

He sighed as the lights dimmed and the music

started. To his surprise, he enjoyed the program. The tenors sang popular songs as well as arias that he recognized. It wasn't a whole opera, just the best parts from several. When it was over, he applauded for an encore with the rest of the crowd.

"That was wonderful," Mary said when they were in Slocum's car, waiting in line to leave the parking lot.

Belle turned in the front seat so she could talk to them. "Colt thought he would hate it, but he clapped louder than anyone for an encore."

"No one likes to hear 'I told you so,'" he groused at her. "But they were good."

"Only the best in the world."

Why hadn't he ever noticed how husky her voice became when she laughed like that? It stroked across his senses like warm honey. It was Belle's laughter, but with something more—a soft, womanly tone that disarmed him.

He shook his head, not liking the direction of his thoughts. He'd tried to ignore her at work all week, but it was impossible. He would walk into the office, returning from a dry, overly long meeting, and there she would be, her radiance lighting the whole reception area.

She and Carmen, who was at least fifty, had become bosom buddies, it seemed. They took their breaks together in Carmen's office, and sometimes ate lunch there. He'd met Kelley Mosher, the personal shopper, last Wednesday, as all three women shared a pizza.

Belle collected people the way a dog picked up fleas. It just happened wherever she went. Even dour old Cheaver, the doorman, smiled and bubbled with cheer when he and Belle arrived home. She was definitely a people person.

"Uh, would you mind if I dropped you and Colt off first?" Slocum asked as he eased into the Friday night traffic.

"Of course not," Belle responded before Colt could.

He frowned in the darkness of the back seat. When playing poker or making a deal, he always got a squirrelly feeling when something wasn't right. He had it now, but he didn't say anything when he and Belle alighted at his place.

Mr. Cheaver rushed to open the door for them, his weathered face wreathed in smiles for Belle.

"Has your daughter thought of a business yet?" Belle asked. "See if Dee needs a partner. I may be looking for something myself."

"What was that all about?" he demanded when they were in the elevator.

She told him about Mr. Cheaver's daughter wanting to start her own company.

"She should look into a reliable housekeeping service," he suggested. "I'm about to fire the one I have."

Belle's eyes lit up. "You may be right. I read that two-thirds of married women now work outside the home. I'll bet they could use someone reliable, too. I'll tell Mr. Cheaver your idea."

Her enthusiasm didn't lift the cloud of anger. He held it in until they were inside the condo. "You're pretty trusting of your lawyer boyfriend to let him take another woman home before you."

"Slocum? He's not my boyfriend. He's my friend. And yes, I trust him completely. He's very sincere." She hung up a black trench coat in the closet, then, yawning, she headed toward the kitchen. "I'm hungry. Are you?"

"No."

"I'm going to have some cocoa. Want some?"

"I suppose."

He followed her, his eyes on the sway of her hips, the straight line of her back, the bounce in her step. A clamor set up in his blood. He stopped her at the kitchen door.

"I don't get you at all," he told her, the anger climbing with each degree of heat that invaded him.

She gave him a wide-eyed look that only fueled his temper. "What is it, Colt?"

"You. Me. I don't know. Except this."

He bent to her lips and this time he didn't stop…couldn't stop…didn't want to stop.…

Belle emitted a squeaky "Oh" just before Colt's mouth crushed down on hers. Her heart slammed around in her chest like a loose ball in a pinball machine.

When his lips touched hers, the first sensation was one of firm strength coupled with gentle warmth. Both the strength and the warmth enveloped her.…

Stunned by the fact that Colt was kissing her, she hadn't taken in the fact that he had also wrapped her in his arms and was holding her as if there was no tomorrow.

His chest formed a solid wall of muscle that pressed and enflamed her breasts into sensitive mounds of yearning. His thighs caressed hers, capturing her legs between his in a stance as intimate as the kiss.

For one terrible second, she thought she might faint and ruin the moment, but she didn't. Instead she wrapped her arms around him and clung to his strength in a world gone mad with wonder.

He released her mouth and let her breathe. His mouth wandered across her cheek to her ear. "Stop me," he ordered, his tone so low and hoarse she could hardly distinguish the words.

Give up this miracle? "No, oh, no."

She clutched a handful of his thick, lustrous hair and refused to let him go. Wild sensation poured over her, and she was filled with need, with hunger that had nothing to do with food and everything with her ravenous heart. It had been so long since anyone had held her....

The next thing she knew she was on the sofa, snuggled safely between the black leather and Colt's hot sinewy length. She'd lost her high heels on the way. She heard two *thunks* as Colt shed his shoes.

He nudged her thighs apart and inserted his knee between them, merging them into the greatest intimacy she'd ever known with a man. It was wonderful and scary and delicious. It was what she'd dreamed of.

"Stop me," he ordered again.

"Never." She moved restlessly against him and felt the solid hardness that told her of his desire.

He wanted her. He really wanted her.

"Show me," she demanded.

His broad, capable, knowing hands raked through

her hair and held her in place while he planted a thousand kisses like a mosaic over her face.

"No," he said with unexpected fierceness.

But he didn't stop.

"Teach me..."

He lifted his head and glared down at her in the muted darkness, lit only by the tiny spotlights in the entryway.

"What do you want to know?" he asked, a note of cruelty in his tone. "How to kiss? You've mastered that."

She felt his stomach muscles contract at his brief laughter. Pushing her hands under his shirt—when had he shed his jacket and tie?—she found his bare skin and caressed urgently along his back.

"Everything," she whispered. "I want to know everything you know."

His breath stopped for a second, then he exhaled roughly and pulled her closer. "This?"

He kissed her mouth.

"This?"

He slipped one hand under her sweater.

"This?"

He moved his hand on her back, then around her side to the front. To her astonishment, her bra was undone.

"This?"

He cupped her breast, his palm against her nipple. Lightning danced along her skin. She shivered as wave after wave of delicious feeling ran through her.

As riotous as she felt physically, her emotions remained in a delicate balance, shifting one way then another as his hands caressed and cajoled a response from her wayward body.

"Is this what you want?" he demanded, his voice a rough, husky growl in her ear as he kissed, then bit, then licked along her neck.

"Yes. No one has ever done this before," she said.

He laughed again, briefly, harshly. "You think not? You are an innocent, aren't you?"

"I meant to me. No one has done this to me. Touch me again." She pressed his hand to her breast, needing his touch more than she needed air.

He rubbed over the entire surface, then plucked gently at her nipple. Ripples of electricity spiraled deep inside, to someplace that was quick and acute and hot with desires that had never been filled.

He went absolutely still. "If you only knew what that knowledge does to a man," he finally said, his breath sighing softly over her temple.

She was surprised by the agony but not the desire in his words. "Does it make you ache?" she asked.

"Yes, it makes me ache. Do you ache, Belle? Do you want more?" It was a challenge.

"Oh, yes, I want everything." She laughed with the sheer joy of being alive in this moment of magic. "I want *you*."

He closed his eyes, but he didn't kiss her. She watched a muscle clench and relax in his jaw. The magic faded.

"Raise up," he urged.

Startled, she sat up. He removed her cardigan and the pullover. The bra slipped down her arms and was discarded someplace behind him on the floor.

"Oh," she breathed when his mouth came down on her breast. He laved his attention on one, then the other for several star-filled moments. She thought she would die of bliss.

"Does this satisfy your curiosity?" he asked.

She stroked his face with fingers that trembled. Looking into his shadowed eyes, she nodded. "The doubts are in you, not me."

He gazed deep into her soul. She returned the look, finding anger and need and other things within him.

She didn't understand those nuances of emotion. She was afraid she wasn't woman enough for him, for the man she sensed inside the controlled, capable being he showed to the world, that she hadn't the experience to reach that man.

Tears filmed her eyes.

He silently kissed them away and licked the salty taste from his lips, his expression softening. "Don't be afraid."

"I'm not," she assured him. "Never of you."

"That's what makes all this so scary. Maybe we should both be afraid." His glance took in their entwined bodies. Before she could answer, he bent to her breasts again. "I'll give you this much, no more."

She didn't know what he meant, but it didn't matter. At last she knew what it was to be held as a woman, to be touched by the one man she wanted more than anyone.

"Oh, Colt, it's so wonderful," she said as he kissed her breasts again. His hands stroked her sides and her back. "I had no idea how wonderful."

He covered her breast with one hand and kissed the corner of her mouth. "Keep talking like that, little virgin, and you may find out just exactly how much better this can get."

She was immediately enchanted. "Show me."

"No."

"Yes." She rubbed against him, thrilling to the hardness of his body against hers.

He cupped her hips and held her. She felt a slight pulsing sensation against her stomach.

"Be still, you little devil." But he was smiling now, as if amused with the whole contretemps between them, as if it was a contest and he had declared himself the winner.

"What happened?" she asked, curious about the change.

"Nothing." At her frown, he added, "You nearly made me lose control. That's something that hasn't happened to me in years. It was...unexpected."

Pride filled her. She smiled and moved against him, experimenting with the heady power of seduction.

He simply rolled his weight forward, holding her pinned to the sofa, while he resumed his slow kisses and caresses, driving her mad while he carefully taught her the difference between a boy's kisses and those of a man.

After several long minutes, he pulled back from their kisses, which had grown steadily hotter. "Rest."

His breathing was quick and deep. He tucked her head against his chest. A button pressed her cheek. Pushing her hands between them, she quickly unfastened the offending material and pushed it out of the way.

Then she discovered she hadn't yet learned all that the tactile sense could teach her. Her breasts, nuzzled in the thick wiry pelt of his chest, experienced entirely new sensations. "Colt, that feels so good," she told him, eagerly exploring this new perception.

He groaned. "You're going to kill me."

She paused. "Does it hurt?"

"Yes, but don't stop. It's a good hurt."

"I want to...you know."

"Yes, but we're not going to. We'll try anything above the waist that you want, but we're not going below. You got that, kiddo?"

He was maintaining a playful mood with her. Well, two could play...

She laid her hand flat against his abdomen. Every muscle in his body contracted into steel. The next thing she knew her hands were pinned above her head and held in one of his while his mouth hovered over hers.

"You'll pay for that trick," he muttered.

Then he proceeded to ravish her, making her moan, making her squirm, at times making her laugh, as he plied his torturous way from mouth to breasts to ticklish torso and back again.

When he let her go and they again rested, their hearts pumping quick and harsh, she said, "I wish the night would never end."

He brushed the hair back from her damp temple. "I thought I was past the time when I could sustain this much passion for hours without fulfilling it. These games are for the young."

"And the back seats of cars parked on a lonely road," she added, smiling at the image.

"How many back seats have you been in?"

"None. My father would have killed anyone who tried to park and make out with me."

He was silent so long she might have thought he was going to sleep except for the tension she could still feel locked within him.

"Is that the real reason you aren't...experienced?"

She pulled the loose edge of his shirt over her

shoulders for warmth as their passion slowly cooled. "Well, I have had some experiences, but they haven't been all that great, you know?"

He frowned. "No. Why don't you tell me? And include names. I'll strangle any guy who hurt you."

"It wasn't that kind of experience. The summer before I turned fourteen, I was invited to a slumber party. The girl's parents weren't home, but I didn't know that. Some boys came over and we played spin the bottle." She looked a question at Colt to be sure he was familiar with the game.

His smile was sardonic. "I'm not that old."

"Okay, so anyway, this boy and I were supposed to kiss, but we were both shy. He gave me a quick one, but his friends weren't having any of that. They made us put our arms around each other. Just as we kissed, someone shoved him. Our braces locked together and we couldn't get apart. They had to call my father. He roused the dentist—it was after midnight by then—and had him meet us at his office in town. It was the most humiliating thing. Everyone for miles knew by morning. That was the last time I got to spend the night with a friend. Dad sent me to the boarding school, and in the summer I was sent on education tours to Europe with old-maid schoolteachers for chaperones."

"One year you threatened to hitch a ride to the ranch and hide there until everyone gave up looking for you."

"Until you talked Dad into letting me come home and then gave me the job of caring for the horses. That was nice of you." She laid her hand flat on his chest and felt the steady beat of his heart against her palm. It was somehow reassuring.

"Yeah. I'm a real hero."

"I wouldn't go *that* far," she teased.

"So what was your next experience?"

"On one of the tours, I fell in love with the Austrian waiter at our hotel. The chaperone caught me with him in a bistro one night. I was sent back to the States. Then came the big mistake."

He raised his eyebrows in question.

"It was Christmas of my senior year. I was feeling rather defiant due to being sent to the all-female college back East instead of living at home and going to the local college. Dad found me and the gardener's son kissing in the garage. He threw the boy out and grounded me for the rest of the holiday."

"Just how intimate was the kiss?"

"Not very."

"This much?" Colt indicated their bare chests still in intimate contact.

She shook her head.

"Were you snuggled up in the back seat of a car?"

"Of course not. We were standing up. The wind blew the door against me and I stepped forward to keep my balance."

"Into his arms?"

"Yes. When I realized he wanted to kiss me, I let him."

"Why?"

She met Colt's level stare with one of her own. "I was curious. I'd never really kissed anyone who wasn't kin to me, except for you and that didn't count. Not then," she added truthfully. "No one in the county dared approach me because of my father. I wanted to see what a real kiss felt like."

"How was it?" Colt tried to shrug off the totally

irrational anger he felt about her kissing some guy in a musty garage.

"Nothing like tonight," she admitted.

He smiled, for once pleased at her blunt honesty. "You could have gotten hurt," he scolded. "If you'd picked the wrong guy and your father hadn't appeared."

"You're saying some men won't take no for an answer. I have a friend from boarding school that happened to. It took her a long time to get over it. She'd trusted him."

"The way you trust me?"

"Yes."

"Maybe you shouldn't put so much faith in a childhood friendship. You're no longer a child."

"There's nothing you could do to break my trust," she protested. "Besides I want you to do everything." Her smile was a challenge meant to provoke him.

His body stirred hungrily, urging him to take all that she offered. "You think you want me, but come morning, you'd have regrets." He forced himself away from her seductive softness and stood. "And so would I."

Ignoring the hurt that leapt into her eyes, he walked away, down the hall and into his bedroom. He closed and locked the door...not against Belle, but as a reminder to himself to stay inside. Alone.

Chapter Five

"If you concentrate in one area, it will save you travel time in going from one place to another," Carmen explained. "That makes your work force more efficient, too, I would think."

"Great idea," Belle agreed.

Colt's secretary had a sharp mind. She was the one who'd suggested they use flyers to spread the word of Dee's new business, Mighty Maids. Dee's father was going to give them out to the residents of Colt's building. She and Carmen were going to distribute them among the businesses in the office building while Kelley was going to put them on the cars at the shopping center during her spare time.

"How can I help?" Mary asked. "An emergency-care clinic probably isn't a good place to solicit housekeeping clients."

"You could make your patients read the flyer before you checked their wounds—like Slocum with his broken collarbone," Belle suggested with a nearly straight face.

Dee giggled. "Right. He might think he's signing a release for you to treat him, but it would really be a contract to get his apartment cleaned."

"He could use some help," Mary assured them.

They laughed in mutual acknowledgement of men's housekeeping abilities.

"I know who your first customer will be. Colt has already asked when you'll start." Belle looked toward the study where their host was ensconced. He'd stayed in there with the door closed most of yesterday and today. "I get to sign him up."

"I'll have to give you a commission," Dee decided. She looked worried. "What if I get more business than I can handle by myself?"

Belle shook her head, amazed at this idea. "You're the boss. You don't do the work. Unless someone fails to show up and you can't get anyone else, of course."

"What do you mean?"

"You're going to hire others to do the work while you handle the business end. You can't do everything."

"Belle's right, Dee," Carmen joined in. "You'll have to schedule the work and handle the contracts and keep things flowing smoothly."

"You shouldn't quit your daytime job yet," Kelley advised. "You'll need a cash flow and money to pay your bills while you're getting established. The reason most new businesses fail is lack of capital. Speaking of which, I'd like to invest in your company if you're interested in a partner. Think about it, and we'll talk later."

"Slocum said he would draw up some sample contracts for you for free," Mary said. "After you're a big success, you can mention his name when you're interviewed by *Forbes* or *Money* magazine for info on how you did it."

Dee fell backward on the floor and covered her face with a flyer. "What if I fail?" She sat up and looked around her group of supporters fearfully.

"You won't," Mary assured her.

Belle thought it over. "To never try would be worse than trying and failing."

"I agree," Kelley said.

"Same here," Carmen added.

Mary nodded her agreement.

Belle and her friends waited while Dee considered.

"You're right," she finally said. "I'll do it. And I'll keep my day job, even if my boss is an obnoxious slimebag."

"But," Belle asked, "is there anything else about him that you don't like?"

Colt hung up the phone and listened to the laughter coming from the kitchen. Belle and her cohorts were busily planning the doorman's daughter's future. She'd asked his advice about the business plan she and Dee Cheaver had written in case Dee needed a loan.

He'd been prepared to be kind. He'd been surprised. The plan was simple but workable. Dee would supply the equipment and thus maintain her self-employed status. As soon as she had enough business for one full month, she'd hire another person and try to grow the market a month at a time. Belle had written the plan.

She was smart and helpful when it came to others. Why didn't she expend the same energy and intelligence on herself to get through college, then take over her interests in their joint businesses?

Belle, like nature, had her own seasons, he concluded. She'd do her own thing in her own time and be damned with anyone who tried to force her into a mold.

He wouldn't have her any other way.

The revelation caused him to pause. He leaned back in the comfortable chair, thoughts of Friday night invading his peace of mind. Peace of mind? He'd had little of that since their wild, senseless episode on the sofa.

He couldn't believe he'd succumbed to passion, allowing it to overrule his wits. His conscience might have drawn a line at the waist, but his mind and body hadn't followed orders. Long after Belle was in bed and asleep, he had tossed restlessly, scenes playing out in his head as he took them both to the farthest reaches of pleasure.

Huffing out a shaky breath, he admitted to the very real temptation to show Belle everything her heart desired. Or thought it did.

No, he wouldn't do that to her. She deserved more. Hal had been right. Belle could marry into any of the prominent families in Texas. She could be more than a roustabout's daughter...or wife.

He was nothing. An orphan. The guy not good enough for a druggist's daughter in a small town. A boy who hadn't had a family or future prospects. He still felt the sting of that rejection even though Belle's mother had told him it was the girl who hadn't been good enough for him.

But it was different now. He could afford cars, penthouses, evenings at the opera. He could afford Marsha and her life-style. A cynical smile pulled at his mouth. Yeah, he could afford the best, but if Marsha was it, he no longer wanted the best.

Belle's laughter pealed out again, piercing the bubble of pain brought on by the past. Belle had once thought he was the greatest. Her trust in him was still a puzzle. Friday night it had almost made him humble.

Grimacing over his body's predictable reaction, he reached for the phone. "Henry?" he said when Slocum's father answered. "The terms are fine. This should be a good deal for both companies. Yeah, and for your son and Belle."

"I think he's seeing another woman. I saw him the other day with someone, but it was from a distance."

"Maybe it was his mother or sister." Belle offered the suggestion to Carmen, who was worried about her daughter.

The secretary's two sons were grown and married, but her daughter, who was twenty-two, was still at home, attending school to become a physical therapist.

"He stood her up two nights last week. To be fair, he called at the last minute and said he couldn't make it. Work was his excuse. I went to a movie with friends. That's when I saw him. When we left the theater, he was down the block, talking very...I don't know...earnestly, maybe, to this woman.''

Belle stuffed a flyer through the mail slot at a law office. Carmen did the same to the one across the hall. They were working during their lunch hour for the third straight day to get Dee's announcements out. So far, she'd gotten few calls, which was a little depressing.

Colt had said to expect a low percent rate of return, that is, three people out of each hundred who got the flyer might call. Of those, maybe two would try the housecleaning service. The ''fighty nuive,'' as they dubbed themselves after Kelley had gotten her tongue twisted on the ''mighty five,'' had decided to expand their base of operations to more office and apartment buildings in the area.

''I need to meet him,'' Belle decided. ''I'm an excellent judge of character. Once my father hired this guy who was a crook. I knew it right off, but would he and Colt listen to me? Of course not.''

''Well, they are men,'' Carmen mentioned. ''As was my former husband, God bless his cheating little heart.''

Belle looked at her companion. Carmen grinned. They burst into laughter and went into the office.

Colt was standing by Carmen's desk. ''I was wondering if you two were going to make it back today.''

''We were distributing Dee's flyers,'' Belle explained. ''We've run out, and we've decided we need to spread the news a little farther. Is it okay if we run off some more on the copier here?''

''Help yourself. No takers yet, huh?'' He was surprisingly sympathetic.

"You're still our only customer." Belle was a little discouraged. "We've distributed almost five hundred flyers. Dee had four calls, but no one has signed up."

"I'll give her a recommendation after I see how she does next week."

"Oh, Colt, would you? That would be so great. We can add a quote from you on the flyer."

"After I see the work," he reminded.

"Dee will do great. I'm going to help her on weekends."

"What?"

"Kelley said Dee shouldn't quit her day job until she was more established, so I told her if she was flooded with work before she could hire some help, I'd help her at night and on weekends."

A forbidding frown settled on Colt's face. "You have too much work to do at the office," he finally announced.

"I wouldn't let it interfere with my learning the business. By the way, when do I get to do something besides answer the phone and file old reports? I'm ready to do some wheeling and dealing."

He snorted, half in amusement, half in exasperation. "When I say you're ready."

Belle made a playful face at him while she tried to judge his mood, which was extremely hard since that passionate interlude on the sofa. He held himself carefully aloof from her, acting more like a cool stranger of late rather than a lifelong friend.

This week she was working with the buyers, updating their catalogs, requesting new ones from companies and generally helping out. She was amazed by the amount of stuff necessary to keep a business running.

She had learned to watch the price of oil, too. With the gulf find, the per-barrel earnings had dropped, which hadn't hurt them since they were the ones in on the kill, so to speak, but that wasn't true for everyone. She'd heard rumors of a shakeout in the industry.

But that was not her problem at the moment. She had work to do and flyers to run off. She went into the small conference room she had been assigned for an office.

Later in the afternoon, Colt entered and closed the door behind him. "I thought you might like to see the financial news," he said mysteriously. He tossed a paper on the table.

Belle picked up the daily newspaper and scanned the headlines. She spotted the news Colt referred to.

"Montbatten declares bankruptcy," she read aloud. She skimmed through the article. "Marsha's father?"

"Yeah." Colt tossed a coin into the air and caught it. He flipped it up again. "You were right. She was looking for the main chance. They needed someone to bail them out...or hang their troubles on."

"Colt, I'm so sorry."

"Yeah, my heart is crushed."

She frowned at his sardonic tone. It wasn't like him to be callous, not really...well, maybe a little...but she was afraid he was using sarcasm as a cover for the pain he must be feeling. Her heart ached for him.

"Do you think she was using you?"

"Yes."

"She might have been in love with you—"

"No, she wasn't."

"Are you terribly hurt?" She went to him and touched his arm in sympathy.

He caught her hand in his, turned it over and studied the palm as if he might deliver a reading of her future.

"Do you realize that by coming to my place when you did you saved me from a fate possibly worse than being forced to eat liver every day for the rest of my life?"

She stared at him, unsure how to take his jest or the hard edge in his voice. He grinned.

She jerked her hand away, her sympathy gone. "You cad. Your heart isn't cracked even a little."

"I realized when Marsha and I had lunch the day after your arrival that it had been a mistake to think of marriage to her. All she wanted to know was how much of Gulfco's assets was mine and how much was yours."

Belle was troubled. "She'll be poor now. For a person used to money, that must be terribly hard."

"Maybe Dee will offer her a job in her new company," he suggested wryly.

"I don't know," she mused aloud. "For someone like me, it's different being poor. I was used to it, and I don't mind doing housework—"

"Belle, Marsha announced her engagement a week ago to some banker friend of her father."

Belle brightened. "Then she'll be all right. Good."

Suddenly he was close, his face only inches from hers. "Sometimes I wonder if you're for real," he murmured.

She stared at him in amazement, her heart fluttering at the intensity in his gaze. "What do you mean?"

"Never mind." He refused to be cajoled or threatened into further discussion.

"Listen, Colt, what would you think of inviting Carmen and her daughter and the daughter's fiancé out to the ranch this weekend?" Belle asked, recalling another topic she wanted to bring up. "Carmen doesn't trust the fiancé. I thought you and I could look him over for her."

"I'm honored that you want my opinion. After all, you're the one who's the instant—and correct—judge of character." He ducked the pencil she threw. "Sure, invite them out. We'll round up cows or something for the dudes."

"I might invite Slocum. And Mary," she said, tossing the words at his retreating form.

He stopped and faced her. "Are you trying to do a little matchmaking between me and Mary? 'Cause if you are, I'm telling you now—forget it."

"No, I'm not, really," she said, able to report with a straight face and a clear conscience.

After another ten seconds of scrutiny, he shrugged. "Invite the whole city. I'm feeling magnanimous."

"That's because you still have that three carat rock."

He laughed. "And I'm going to keep it."

Belle rolled her eyes, then got back to work. That evening, she called everyone she wanted to have at the ranch for the weekend. She was sure Colt wouldn't mind the one or two extra people she invited.

"Sure, I'll grill the steaks. What else do I need to do?" Colt asked on the way to the ranch on Friday night.

The twilight had deepened into dark. They'd been stuck in freeway traffic for over an hour due to an accident on their way out of the city. They were almost home, and Belle was bringing him up-to-date on her plans for the weekend.

"Nothing. I've talked to Ginny Taylor at the ranch and she's making salads and desserts. I've brought some of that wonderfully crunchy sourdough bread from the bakery. The foreman is getting beer and cola. I thought we might take a ride to the cascades late tomorrow afternoon, then get back to the house for dinner around eight."

"All right."

"You're being awfully agreeable about this." She gave him a suspicious glance from the corner of her eye.

Like her, Colt had changed to jeans and a long-sleeved shirt for the drive out of town. She eased the seat belt out, then shifted sideways so she could study him more easily.

"What?" he finally said.

"I was wondering if you were going to kiss me again."

His expression slid into a scowl. "No."

"If you were interested in a woman, what would you do? I mean, how would you let her know?"

He shot her an oblique glance, one dark eyebrow quirking upward in sardonic amusement. "Curious about how I do my courting, Belle?"

"Yes," she admitted, unabashed by his cutting tone. "What did you do when you and Marsha met?"

"She asked me to a party at her house. Then I asked her out to dinner. Later I took her to a charity ball—"

"Was that your idea or hers?"

He considered. "Hers, now that you mention it."

"I don't think she's a good example. Who did you date before that?"

"An accountant I had when I opened this office. That's a mistake I'll never make again. Never date anyone who works in the same office."

"Well, I know that. A boss should never get involved with an employee. Or an employee's son with the boss's daughter. Dad fired the gardener whose son kissed me and wouldn't give him a reference. I felt terrible about him losing his job because of me."

Colt pulled into the garage and killed the engine. He unsnapped the seat belt, then studied Belle before getting out. "If Hal were alive and found out I kissed you last Friday, he would probably hog-tie and hang me."

"I'm almost twenty-one. I handle my own affairs."

"Or lack of them?" Colt suggested. He pushed open the car door and headed inside without waiting for her answer.

She grimaced at his back and followed, bringing her overnight case. "Not from want of trying," she snapped, then remembered that he knew all about her past mishaps.

He held the door and caught a strand of her hair as she entered, stopping her on the threshold. "Poor Belle. What was that line you quoted once from a Greek play, something about going to your grave unwept, unsung and…unkissed? No, hardly that. But still a curious virgin.''

His breath touched her temple as he murmured his wickedly teasing words. She shivered at his dark mood, finding it thrilling and dangerous and seductive.

She caressed his cheek. ''Did you ever stop to wonder why women always fall for black-hearted rogues?''

His smile widened. ''Tell me.''

''Because it's so much fun when we bring them to their knees. Someday you'll beg for my kisses.''

He took her hand and lightly kissed each fingertip before he spoke. ''Watch out. Children who play with matches sometimes get burned.''

''Or maybe we'll start a fire that won't be put out.''

To her chagrin, he burst into laughter. ''Yes, there is that problem,'' he agreed, and ushered her into the house.

''This is lovely,'' Kelley exclaimed, examining the ranch with a fashion buyer's eye for color and line.

Belle smiled absently in acknowledgment. She was mulling over the sleeping arrangements. She had planned to put Carmen and her daughter, Leah, in one room, Slocum and Jamie and Leah's CPA fiancé, Darrel, in another—the Taylor boys had set up bunk beds at her request—and Kelley and Mary in her room while she took the sofa in Colt's study.

However, Carmen had come down with the flu and been unable to join them, Slocum had asked if he and Mary could share a room, and Kelley had indicated she and Jamie would prefer to be together.

If she put Leah and the CPA together, then it would work out. But what if he turned out to be terrible?

She wouldn't want to be accused of aiding and abetting the affair by Carmen. She had better put Darrel on the sofa.

Still frowning, she went to see about lunch. Colt was in the kitchen, talking to Ginny, when she entered.

"Why the big frown?" he asked.

"I was just thinking life must have been easier in the olden days, like when you were young," she said to him with her most innocent look, "and sleeping arrangements were easier to figure out."

Ginny smothered a laugh in a fit of coughing.

Colt gave her a wicked leer. "You can sleep with me if you've lost your bed."

"Ha, you wish."

The foreman's wife didn't look the least shocked by Colt's suggestion. Belle wondered how many other women he'd shared his bed with on a cozy weekend visit. That left her feeling decidedly grumpy during lunch and afterward when Colt gave them a tour of the ranch.

Her spirits picked up when they were saddled and on their way across the broad pastures to the cascades. Colt kept the pace to an easy walk so that even the most tender of city slickers wouldn't have difficulty. She chafed at the restraint.

"Restless?" he inquired when she let her mount overtake his and go in front.

She reined in. "I'd like a run."

"See if anyone wants to join you. I'll hold the others in check." He dropped back to Leah and took hold of her bridle and the one to Kelley's mare. "Belle wants to go for a run if anyone wants to do the same. Otherwise, hold your mount back until the others are gone."

Mary clicked her mount to a trot, then a canter and joined Belle. Slocum joined them. "Race you to the oak growing out of that rock."

"You're on," Mary shouted, and took off.

Belle and Slocum leaned forward. Their horses surged into action. Mary urged her mare faster. Belle laughed, her hair mingling with the dark mane that whipped along her cheek as she rode hell-for-leather across the pasture. She left Slocum and caught up with Mary.

Mary shouted and fanned the mare with the reins. She, too, stretched out along her steed's neck.

Belle loved it. The calls behind them, the pounding of the animal's shod hooves, their laughter, all disappeared until there existed only the moment and the feel of the horse under her, the wind against her ears. She felt fiercely, joyously alive, as if all of life came down to *now* and the excitement of the race between her and her friend.

The oak tree loomed ahead, then came alongside, then disappeared behind them. She was half a nose ahead. Laughing with triumph, she pulled up, knowing the creek and the boulders were directly over the next swell of land.

Mary didn't. Elated, she urged her mount to continue. Too late she heard Belle's shout of warning. The horse took the first plunging steps down the bank and into the creek. It went down on its knees. Mary pitched forward.

"Mary," Belle shouted as her friend disappeared into the water, her head striking one boulder, then another.

She urged the mare forward into the frothing water and let the surefooted cow pony find her way toward Mary. When they came abreast, Belle leapt to a rock and grabbed Mary's shirt and hauled her up out of the water.

Slocum arrived at the same moment and lifted her into his arms, then carried her to the bank. Belle grabbed the loose horses and tied them to one side while Slocum and Colt, who had quickly reached their side, examined her friend. She returned, feeling remorseful about suggesting the run.

"I'm okay," Mary said, sitting up and leaning heavily against Slocum. "It wasn't your fault," she said to Belle. "I should have stopped when you shouted."

"I thought you didn't hear me." Belle crouched down and surveyed her friend. "You've got a bruise on your forehead and a cut in your scalp that needs stitches."

"How many fingers am I holding up?" Slocum asked. He pressed his handkerchief to the cut to stop the bleeding.

"Two. Really, I'm fine. Just a bit woozy."

"Slocum and I will decide that," Colt told her in no uncertain terms. "I'll ride back and bring the car out. We'll get her to the local sawbones."

Mary gave up arguing and let herself be taken care of. Belle dipped Slocum's handkerchief in the icy water and bathed Mary's bruises and checked her eyes to see if her pupils were the same size.

"I don't think you have a concussion, but the cut needs to be cleaned and sewn up."

It was dark when Colt returned to the ranch with Slocum and Mary sitting in the front seat of the car. She had four neat stitches in her scalp, an ice pack on her shoulder and a bandage on her elbow.

Belle had asked Jamie and Darrel to take over cooking the steaks. They were ready, as was everything else. Now she set about putting the food on the long table in the ranch dining room. Kelley and Leah helped her. They'd all been rather silent since the accident.

Belle still felt terrible. She was relieved to see the big grin on Mary's face when the three arrived from the doctor's visit. She made Mary take the most comfortable chair. Colt had her prop her feet up. Slocum brought her a cup of hot tea.

"Hey, I could get used to this," Mary declared. "I would make a great tyrant. Another spoon of sugar," she ordered Slocum, drawing a laugh from the others when they saw she was really all right.

Colt came into the dining room and helped Belle set the table. "Don't beat yourself up over it," he advised.

She looked a question at him.

"You always took more than your share of the blame when something went wrong."

"I wanted to run."

"I told you to do it."

"I should have warned her beforehand."

"She should have listened when you did."

Belle stopped protesting her guilt. He smiled at her. Her heart eased some. She smiled, too.

Something bright kindled in his eyes. For a moment she saw the old warmth in those cool gray eyes. She took a step toward him, needing his arms around her and his comforting touch after the hours of worry. She stopped as the gray lost its warmth and became frosty again.

"We'd better feed the city slickers before they decide to slaughter a cow themselves," he said.

Chapter Six

Colt watched the activity in the living room after dinner with a jaundiced eye. Slocum was paying entirely too much attention to Mary. At the moment, he sat on the floor at Mary's feet, surfing through the television programs in search of a movie she wanted to watch. All evening he'd waited on the woman as if she were fragile...or as if he were in love with her. It bothered him on account of Belle.

Not that she seemed in the least disturbed.

However, he knew that she tended to conceal her own pain and take on other people's concerns and battles. It was part and parcel of her generous nature. He didn't want to see her hurt.

The light gleamed on her hair as she bent over a jigsaw puzzle she and Kelley had started. Leah, the CPA and Jamie were also working on it, all seated around the table and as busy as elves. Empty popcorn bowls rested on the windowsill and various small tables.

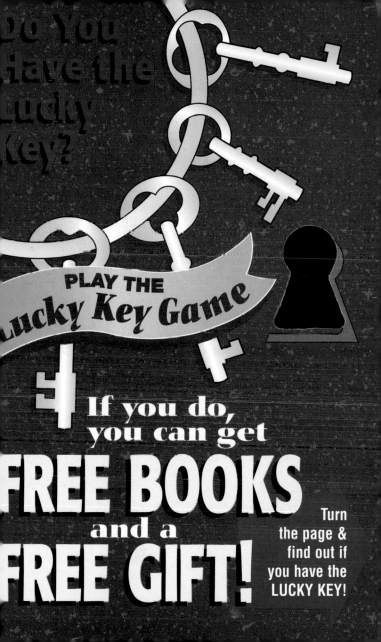

HOW TO PLAY:

1. With a coin, carefully scratch off gold area at the right. Then check the claim chart to see what we have for you — **FREE BOOKS** and a **FREE GIFT** — **ALL YOURS FREE!**

2. Send back this card and you'll receive brand-new Silhouette Romance™ novels. These books have a cover price of $3.50 each, but they are yours to keep absolutely free.

3. There's no catch. You're under no obligation to buy anything. We charge nothing — ZERO — for your first shipment. And you don't have to make any minimum number of purchases — not even one!

4. The fact is thousands of readers enjoy receiving books by mail from the Silhouette Reader Service™ months before they're available in stores. They like the convenience of home delivery and they love our discount prices!

5. We hope that after receiving your free books you'll want to remain a subscriber. But the choice is yours — to continue or cancel, any time at all! So why not take us up on our invitation, with no risk of any kind. You'll be glad you did!

YOURS FREE!
A SURPRISE MYSTERY GIFT

We can't tell you what it is...but we're sure you'll like it! A
FREE GIFT—
just for playing the
LUCKY KEY game!

FREE GIFTS!

NO COST! NO OBLIGATION TO BUY!
NO PURCHASE NECESSARY!

The Silhouette Reader Service™ — Here's how it works:

Accepting free books places you under no obligation to buy anything. You may keep the books and gift and return the shipping statement marked "cancel." If you do not cancel, about a month later we'll send you 6 additional novels and bill you just $2.90 each, plus 25¢ delivery per book and applicable sales tax, if any.* That's the complete price — and compared to cover prices of $3.50 each — quite a bargain! You may cancel at any time, but if you choose to continue, every month we'll send you 6 more books, which you may either purchase at the discount price...or return to us and cancel your subscription.

*Terms and prices subject to change without notice. Sales tax applicable in N.Y.

If offer card is missing write to: Silhouette Reader Service, 3010 Walden Ave., P.O. Box 1867, Buffalo, NY 14240-1867

BUSINESS REPLY MAIL

FIRST-CLASS MAIL   PERMIT NO. 717   BUFFALO, NY

POSTAGE WILL BE PAID BY ADDRESSEE

SILHOUETTE READER SERVICE
3010 WALDEN AVE
PO BOX 1867
BUFFALO NY 14240-9952

NO POSTAGE
NECESSARY
IF MAILED
IN THE
UNITED STATES

He experienced a strange contraction in his chest as he studied the homey scene. Belle was able to turn any condo or house...or office...into a home or caring place. She knew everyone who worked for him right down to the janitor, whose wife had had surgery for breast cancer recently. Belle had a word and a smile for everyone.

He frowned when Slocum went to the kitchen and refilled Mary's cup of tea. At eleven, they watched the news and decided to go to bed. He waited until the room was empty then turned out the lights.

Restless, he prowled the study before settling on a techno thriller he'd been meaning to read. Belle looked surprised when she found him there. She carried a pillow and blanket with her.

"What are you doing?" he asked.

"I was going to sleep on the sofa. I'll take the one in the living room."

"You can stay in here. I'm ready to go to bed. Who's in your room?"

"Mmm, Kelley and Jamie, I think. I sort of left it to them to figure it out."

"I suppose Leah and Darrel are sharing?"

"Yes. What did you think of him?"

Colt shrugged. "He's okay. For an accountant."

She beamed. "I think so, too. Carmen will be so relieved when I tell her. But there is something mysterious about Darrel. I'll try to find out what he's hiding. I think he has a problem."

"Where's Slocum sleeping?"

"I think he put one of the bunk bed mattresses on the floor somewhere," she replied with a vague gesture. She tossed the pillow and blanket on the sofa.

Something wasn't adding up. There wasn't another room upstairs for Slocum. Was he sleeping in the hall? Curious, Colt left Belle and silently stole up the stairs.

No Slocum on the floor. He wasn't in the bathroom. Colt eyed the room assigned to Mary. Feeling like a cat burglar, he crept close and pressed his ear to the wood.

He heard Mary speak, then a deeper rumble. Definitely a male voice. He clenched his hands into fists and itched to burst into the room. Drawing a calming breath, he eased away and down the stairs.

The door to the study was closed. Belle was probably in bed. Good. He didn't want to see her. Not before he had a talk with the Casanova upstairs.

Unable to settle, he went into the kitchen and heated a cup of leftover coffee in the microwave. Moonlight played hide-and-seek with the clouds, scattering shadows over the meadow where the cows bunched in the night wind.

He could remember being nineteen and longing for the comfort of a home so desperately he'd thought he would die of loneliness. Then Hal and Lily had taken him in. He'd spent every holiday with the Glamorgans since that time.

Even after he'd rejected Belle's offer of marriage and herself, she'd still included him at Christmas and Easter, the Fourth of July and Thanksgiving without fail. He wouldn't stand idly by and let some guy use her for his own nefarious purposes.

A fiercely protective fury rose in him. Belle's affections weren't to be taken lightly. He would tell that to the lawyer.

A noise broke into his seething thoughts. He turned to find the object of his anger entering the kitchen. Slocum smiled and nodded.

"I thought I'd get a fresh pitcher of water and set it on the table beside Mary in case she needs to take a pill during the night," he said.

"What the hell are you up to?" Colt demanded, fighting a need to toss the scoundrel up against the wall and beat the living tar out of him.

The younger man set the pitcher on the counter and cast Colt a puzzled glance. "Uh, I assumed it would be okay if I got some ice water."

"What the hell are you doing in the room with Mary?" Colt bore down on the sneaky bastard until he stood within hitting distance.

"Oh," Slocum said, grinning as if all had suddenly become clear to him. "I moved one of the mattresses from a bunk to the floor in there. I didn't want to take a chance of jostling her during the night."

"So, you are sleeping with her. And with Belle in the study. Dammit, she believes in you. She thinks you're sincere, but I knew you and Mary were more than friends."

Something in the pitch of his tone finally rung through to the blockhead. "I don't see that the situation between me and Mary is any of your business."

Colt considered the pleasure he would get in pounding the guy to a pulp. "I'm making it mine." He flashed Slocum a slow, evil grin of anticipation. "You want to step outside?"

"Good Lord, no. It's dark out. And I'm barefoot."

He inched toward the doorway as if planning a dash up the stairs and to safety.

"So am I. Meet me in the stable in five minutes. Don't make me have to come get you." Colt stalked out and went into his bedroom.

"Belle, you in here?"

Belle, having just that second drifted into sleep, nearly jumped off the sofa. "Slocum? Is Mary okay?" She sat up and switched on the lamp.

Slocum looked behind him, then closed the door. "Your friend has gone bonkers," he said, coming over to the sofa. He ran a hand through his rumpled hair.

"Mary?" she asked, astounded and worried about what might have happened. "A concussion? We'll call an—"

"Not Mary. Colter McKinnon."

"Colt? What's wrong with him?"

"He just threatened to beat me up. He did," Slocum insisted at her incredulous stare. "He said to meet him in the stable in five minutes. Or else he'd come after me."

"Colt?"

"Yeah."

"Colt said that?"

"*Yes.*"

She threw back the blanket. "I'd better go see about him. In the stable?"

"Yeah. I...uh...think he thinks there's something between me and Mary, and that I'm...uh, not being true to you or something."

She slipped her feet into her loafers while Slocum

beat a trail back up the stairs. After hesitating, she decided to check Colt's room first. Nope, he wasn't there. Shaking her head at his crazy notion, she grabbed a mackinaw from a chair and headed outside.

The wind was chilly and seemed to blow right through her clothes to her bones. She pulled the heavy wool jacket tight around her neck. She sniffed the sleeve and recognized Colt's scent along with that of the horses and hay.

She entered the stable from a side door. "Colt?"

"That coward," he snarled out of the darkness, "sending a woman instead of facing me himself."

"What are you ranting about? Slocum thinks you've gone bonkers. I'm going to have to agree if you don't tell me what this is about."

He gave her a snarly glance, then loosened his fists and rammed his hands into his pockets. "Nothing."

"You want to fight a guest in the middle of the night and it's nothing?" She sighed, exasperated with him. "Colt, Slocum is my friend. That's all."

"Ha. Some friend," he muttered.

She saw she would have to confess all. "He and Mary are in love, but his parents disapprove of her. She's seven years older than Slocum. She's divorced, but her husband left her with a large credit card debt before he bailed out. They think she's after money."

An ominous frown creased the line between his brows. "So what about you and him?"

"Well, we sort of pretended to date so that his dad would get off his back while he convinced Mary to take a chance on him. She thinks she's not right for him, too."

"So the double-dating and you and him going out every night was a cover for them to see each other?"

She smiled brightly when he caught on so quick. "Right. He told me about it that night when you had his father over for the cocktail party—"

"So you've been in on it from the first?"

"Yes." She moved a step back, then another.

Colt followed, his eyes narrowed into slits. "Why am I not totally shocked to hear this?" he asked softly. "Because Belle Glamorgan is involved," he answered. "Because wherever there's trouble, there's sure to be Belle, doing her bit to aid romance, female entrepreneurs or the down-and-out."

She felt the door at her back. She reached behind her for the latch, found it, eased it up. "Well, now that we have this cleared up, I think we should go to bed. Colt, I'm so sorry. I should have explained—"

"Not at all. It isn't your way. You let me and Slocum's father think all was wonderful between you. I told him it was. He has all but ordered the champagne and reserved a hotel for the wedding."

He lunged for her. She broke and ran, leaving him grabbing the door as she banged it closed behind her. She made it to the study and slammed the door. She didn't lock it. No force on earth could keep Colt out if he was determined to get in.

Five minutes passed.

Another.

Belle sat on the sofa, the blanket huddled around her while she waited. Ten minutes passed. She heard Colt enter the house and go to his room. He closed the door loud enough for her to hear, but not enough to alarm their guests.

After another ten minutes, she decided she was safe. She flung his jacket over a chair and snuggled into the pillow. There would be the devil to pay tomorrow. And his name was Colter McKinnon.

To her surprise, Colt was smiling and relaxed. At breakfast he spoke to Slocum. "I apologize for last night. I was under a misconception. Belle straightened me out."

"No problem," Slocum said with a relieved smile. "Uh, Mary and I have an announcement. I have finally convinced her that life is too short and too uncertain not to take the good parts when they're offered. She has agreed to become my wife. We've set the date for July the seventeenth."

Belle burst into laughter. She raced around the table to give the bridal couple hugs and kisses. "Do you realize that's not far off? We'll have to start planning now to get everything done. I know the perfect place to order the cake. Monsieur Pierre makes the best desserts."

"See?" Slocum told Mary. "I told you Belle would have some suggestions. That sounds great," he said to Belle. "Where can we hold the ceremony? We don't have much money."

"In the park by the river? I know someone with the most gorgeous roses. She'll let us have all we want."

For the rest of the long weekend, they planned the wedding. Colt offered to host the reception at the country club. "Consider it a peace offering," he said.

He and Slocum exchanged grins.

The next day was the Fourth of July. After a picnic

and local fireworks by the county fire department, their guests headed back for the city. Belle packed and waited while Colt talked to his foreman about the ranch.

The cows grazed peacefully with their calves, she noted, watching a couple of young ones in the meadow. She had a sense of time passing swiftly. She'd been living with Colt for a month. She pressed a hand between her breasts, her breath a sharpness in her chest as longing rose.

"What is it?" Colt asked, entering the kitchen and standing behind her at the window.

She ached with the possibility of life, an anticipation of the future that was buried deep in her female genes.

"I was thinking of life, of having children," she added softly.

Colt's lungs stopped working. His heart gave a giant lurch. Blood pooled into a hot tumescence in his loins. He carefully inhaled and exhaled until he was sure he had his body under control before he spoke.

"All six of them?" he asked lightly, teasing about her declaration that she wanted a half-dozen kids with him.

She glanced over her shoulder and smiled, then returned to her contemplation of the ranch land.

He was intensely aware of her as a female. And of how ethereal she suddenly seemed, this Belle who was, yet wasn't, the girl he'd always known.

A pensive aura surrounded her, enveloping her in mysterious womanhood. She seemed ethereal, but he was aware that she was real...alive...warm... responsive.

When he put his hands on her shoulders, she leaned against him, lightly touching his chest. Heat ran to the area, and his skin tingled. He wanted... He didn't know what he wanted.

The old Belle, the child who was as readable as a page in a book, who loved life and adored him?

Or this new Belle, a stranger he glimpsed from time to time, one with nuances and moods he couldn't identify, the one who stirred him to passion so wild he'd nearly lost his head while kissing her?

"Nothing can stay the same forever," he said, speaking his thoughts aloud.

"Would you want it to?"

There was a wealth of wisdom in the question and a knowledge that went eons beyond Belle's twenty years on earth. He sensed she was involved in other mysteries as she stood quietly and watched the calves gamboling in the grass.

A sense of loss hit him.

She was gone—his Belle, his sweet childish companion who had shared every thought with him. Here, in her place, was this woman—hauntingly familiar, strangely different, new and enchanting.

It confused him. It made him angry.

And that was the most confusing of all.

She turned abruptly and stepped away. "Ready?"

"Yeah." He grabbed his jacket and car keys, then led the way to the garage.

Once on the road, he felt relief, as if he had stumbled close to an abyss and only an act of fate had kept him from tumbling over the dark edge into the unknown.

* * *

"What do you think?" Kelley adjusted the fold of white satin and stepped back.

"Too lovely for words," Belle said, pressing her hands together at her breast. "Mary, that's it."

"I don't feel right in white. I'm not a virgin." Mary fingered the beautiful material, her face filled with longing and uncertainty.

"No one pays any attention to that nowadays," Kelley assured her. "Ninety-nine percent of all brides would have to marry in some other color."

Belle gave Mary a comforting pat. "White is for purity. You love Slocum and want only the best for him. That's purity of heart, the most important kind."

Tears filmed Mary's blue eyes. "Do you think his father was terribly angry when Slocum told him?"

Belle nodded. "But it doesn't matter. Only you and Slocum can decide how much you're going to let him influence your lives. You two have to set the boundaries. Mr. Walters has to respect them. If he doesn't, then you must limit his contact with your family."

"Slocum is looking for a position at a law firm. He's decided to move out of his father's business."

"Good."

"I feel so guilty," Mary explained. "As if I'm tearing Slocum's family apart."

Kelley squatted and pinned a tuck into the skirt of the bridal gown. She shook her head thoughtfully. "They're doing it to themselves. And I guess we let them."

Belle and Mary looked at each other, then Kelley.

She sat on the floor cross-legged and methodically pinned the hem in place. "Look at us—me, Mary and Leah, too. The parents are trying to decide who should be included in our lives, who should be important to us, but they aren't the ones who are living alone and unhappy. We are."

"You're right," Belle said. "If we checked, what do you want to bet that *their* parents didn't like their choices? You would think they might learn to let people live their own lives. And that includes making their own mistakes."

"Be happy," Kelley told Mary. She grinned. "That's the best revenge."

Mary sighed. "You two make me feel so much better. Has anyone heard from Dee this week?"

"Oh, yes," Kelley said on a brighter note. "Dee had over fifty calls over the weekend. She said she couldn't put the phone down. She has thirty-two customers signed up for a three-month introductory service. She's hired two women, housewives who want to work part-time. We're going to be partners and have a schedule set up for sharing the work."

"She did a great job at Colt's condo. The questionnaire on what the customer wants done was brilliant—"

"Ahem," said Kelley, polishing her nails on her blouse in self-congratulation on her brilliance.

"And Slocum's idea for the three-month introductory offer was also good," Belle told Mary, giving Kelley a playful kick.

"What was the thing between Slocum and Colt?" Kelley asked. "Did they have words?"

Mary and Belle smothered laughter. Belle explained. "Colt thought Slocum was playing me false when he found him up in Mary's bedroom."

"Colt invited Slocum outside," Mary added, looking more than a little shocked by this barbaric behavior.

"To the stable, actually," Belle corrected. "I went out and told him to stop acting like a dolt."

"Hmm." Kelley leaned back on her arms and studied Belle. "Very protective of his one chick, isn't he?"

Belle sighed. "He thinks he has to keep an eye on me, or else I'll get lost crossing the street."

"Parents, again," Kelley moaned, getting back to her task. "Honestly. Jamie and I are about ready to write ours off. We told them we were seeing each other, and they could like it or lump it."

"Good for you." Belle picked up the clipboard she'd brought with her to the store for the fitting. "Now back to business. Did you think of any other names you want to add to the guest list?"

"My great-aunt said she would come." Mary groaned. "How do you keep a wedding small when you're kin to the whole state of Texas?"

Belle stood at the window of the penthouse and watched the cars and pedestrians rush through the driving rain of a Texas thundershower. Friday-night traffic was worse than usual. Colt hadn't yet arrived home. He'd been out of the office, meeting with lawyers all day.

She sighed and gazed at the clouds as lightning raced through them and sometimes to the ground. Like the darkening sky, her mood was edgy and restless. The fitting for Mary's wedding dress at noon had left her with longings she couldn't name. They pierced her heart, leaving her wretched and lost.

Maybe she wanted too much from life. The odd thing was she couldn't even express what it was she longed for so fervently. Just that she felt it...and it hurt.

Hearing a key in the lock, she turned and waited for Colt to appear. Kelley had indicated Colt guarded her as a mother hen would a chick, but Belle was sure he didn't look upon her as a parent or older brother might. Not after that night on the sofa.

Her heart raced out of control as memory flooded her senses with all the wondrous sensations she'd experienced with him—the heat of their intermingled bodies, the scent of her cologne and his aftershave, the prickly caress of his chest against her breasts, the brush of his hands, the roaming of his lips....

Fierce, unexpected pain swept over her. She knew what she longed for. And that she would never have it.

She loved Colter McKinnon. It was that simple. Not with the slavish adoration she'd felt for him while growing up, but with a woman's love and all the longing for home and family that coursed through her like a never-ending river, stretching far into the past and all the women who'd come before her, reaching out to the future and those daughters who would come after her.

Colt and her love for him were the center of that dream.

With sudden insight, she knew Colt wrapped his innermost self in armor plating. A maverick in the oil fields, a rogue in business, cool and clear thinking and bold, he guarded his heart as carefully as a warrior in battle. That was why he had considered marriage to a woman he couldn't possibly love.

The hopelessness of loving him beat at her the way the rain beat at the windowpane, with no hope of penetrating to the warmth beyond.

He entered in his usual brisk manner, a man with things to do and people to see. He seemed to know precisely what he was doing and where he was going. She wished she had a solid sense of direction, a place to go, a place to belong....

"Something smells good," he said, a smile lighting his angular face. To her, he was incredibly handsome.

"Dinner is ready. I fixed barbecued chicken like Mom used to make." She'd drifted into the habit of preparing their evening meal. There were only so many times a week she could stand pizza or Chinese takeout.

"Great. Okay if I change first?"

"Yes. I'll need ten minutes to set the table."

He nodded and hurried down the hall to his room. She put the meal on the table, her thoughts on the past and the times they were together—her mom and dad, Colt and herself.

The familiar tug of homesickness engulfed her. She knew it well from those first days, weeks, months at boarding school when all she'd dreamed of was returning to a home that no longer existed, when she'd cried secretly at night for a mother who could no longer comfort her.

She finished her task just as Colt returned to the kitchen in cutoffs and a blue T-shirt that lent a touch of blue to his eyes. His legs were tanned and muscular. He was barefoot.

For some reason that made her heart ache all over again. She took her seat when he did.

"Chicken, potato salad, baked beans, jalapeño corn bread," he said in pleased surprise. "My favorites. Your mom always invited me over for supper when she fixed this."

"You and Dad could eat a whole chicken each." Tears filmed her eyes. She had to quit remembering, quit longing for impossible things.

"Working in the oil fields built up an appetite. Sometimes I miss that. A person never had to worry about going to a gym to get enough exercise. Somehow it seems more honest to get your muscles in real work."

She tried not to stare while they ate, but she couldn't seem to take her eyes off Colt. Each time he looked up, she quickly stared at her plate, but soon her eyes were drawn back to him.

He glanced up and met her gaze. A questioning frown settled on his brow. "What is it?"

Leaping to her feet, she removed the plates from the table. "We have dessert. Banana pudding."

He chuckled. "If you're buttering me up for something, it's working. I haven't had banana pudding since—" He stopped abruptly. "Belle?"

"Yes?" She brought the treat to the table and took her chair. She picked up her spoon.

"Look at me," he ordered softly.

For a moment she was afraid the misery would spill over in hot tears. But it didn't. Instead she summoned a smile and looked directly at him.

His frown deepened. He gestured toward the empty

plates. "I've been thoughtless," he said. "You're thinking of your mother."

Belle shook her head. "It's not that. It was... Mary tried on her wedding dress today. She was so beautiful."

He was silent while they finished the dessert, then he helped her clean up the kitchen. When she went into the living room, he followed instead of going to his study as he'd been doing nearly every night.

She stood at the window and watched the rain. In the reflection of the room, she saw Colt fold his sinewy frame onto one of the black leather sofas.

"Did you pick out the furnishings in here?" she asked, studying the black lacquer-and-glass tables, the modular chairs and lamps. She couldn't see Colt in a furniture store picking out the ultramodern decor.

"No. Some designer did it for the builder. He offered the stuff to me when I bought the place. Why?"

"It's too impersonal for a home." She turned to him. "I shouldn't have said that. It's none of my business."

He grinned, and she realized he could look endearing.

"You've never let that stop you when you thought I needed to know something." He chuckled.

She turned back to the storm.

"You're moody tonight." He spoke directly behind her, his hands settling lightly on her shoulders.

"It's nothing. The rain, the storm..."

"You used to like them. When you were a kid, Lily could hardly keep you inside during a storm."

"When I was a kid," she echoed.

Colt sensed something in Belle, a sadness he'd

never found before, not even after Lily died and Belle had clung to him, her young body trembling with the force of her grief. This was different, but he couldn't say how. Belle was hurting, and for the first time, he didn't know why or how to help.

He rubbed her shoulders and massaged her neck. At last, the coiled tension began to unwind. She sighed and rested her forehead against the window.

"I think I'd better move to a place of my own," she said.

The anger hit him first. He turned her to face him. "No," he said fiercely, meaning it.

She didn't flinch. "Yes."

He didn't know why, but the next thing he did was kiss her.

Chapter Seven

Belle's first reaction was one of surprise and wild delight, then she gave herself to the kiss with all the fierce passion in her heart.

She felt Colt's hesitation, then his arms swept around her and brought her close. His muscles tensed as if he waged an unseen battle, then he shuddered and drew her closer until they touched everywhere along the curves and planes of their bodies. His lips were rapacious on hers, taking her by storm, and yet...the gentleness, always the underlying gentleness, the controlled strength, the sense of caring she got from him....

The tears seeped onto her face and ran down to their locked mouths. He moved his head, his lips roaming hungrily over hers, then he paused.

Colt tasted the saltiness of her tears and groaned deep in his throat. He didn't want tears. He wanted passion. He wanted the mindless release of their bodies locked together. He wanted to be less shocked by his reaction to her.

This was Belle, the girl—woman—he was sworn to protect. He was supposed to guide her into a suitable marriage, not seduce her. He'd given his word.

Belle can do better'n a couple of roustabouts like us, eh, lad?

Yeah, a hell of a lot better.

It was the hardest thing to do, but he forced himself away from her. She watched him warily, her eyes shadowed with thoughts he couldn't read.

"This can never be," he said.

A flicker of emotion ran through her eyes, then was gone. He thought it might have been pain.

"I would never hurt you," he murmured.

"Not intentionally."

The wry tilt to her smile puzzled and intrigued him. he caressed her cheek lightly. "But you think I would without meaning to. How?"

"When you kiss me, then remember I'm Belle. And that you don't want me."

He cupped her face between his hands. "Little fool. I shake from wanting you. I can't sleep from thinking about how it could be between us."

She shook her head. "I don't believe you. Show me," she challenged. She smiled in the impish way that delighted and annoyed him. "Dare you."

"No."

But it was damned hard to resist when she swayed against him like a willow sapling in the wind, lithe and supple and...looking into the hazy sensual heat reflected in her eyes...passionate.

When had Belle become beautiful?

And sexy?

She moved against him, a light, teasing stroke of her body against his. Heat roared into an inferno of hunger, and more than hunger, a need that reached inside to a place that hadn't been touched in years. That place was raw and sensitive and much too vulnerable to be exposed.

"No," he said again. This time he meant it. He stepped back, then spun and left the room and the storm that raged inside and outside.

"Darrel broke a date Saturday night with Leah," Carmen told Belle while they took a coffee break at Carmen's desk.

Belle, who had been put in charge of finding the best deals on household supplies—the bathroom brigand, as she called herself—finished a doughnut and licked her fingers.

"Hmm, I wish we could find a way to follow him when he does that. I'm sure he's in love with Leah, but there's something disturbing him. He was distracted at times at the ranch. He's worried."

"If he has some deep dark secret, I'd like Leah to know it before they marry. A bride has enough to cope with without any extra unpleasant surprises."

"You mean the way men leave their underwear and socks on the floor beside the bed all the time? And they don't rinse the stubble down the drain when they shave?"

"My ex channel surfed until I wanted to hit him with the remote control."

Belle laughed. "Colt does that. It's a guy thing. He says he can watch several sports shows that way."

Carmen gave her a quizzical glance. "Does he leave his underwear on the floor beside his bed?"

"I don't know. I'm not privy to his bedroom." Belle sighed glumly.

"But you'd like to be?"

Belle wasn't ready to admit that much.

"You're in love," the secretary said softly, checking Colt's door to make sure it was closed.

"A woman would be foolish to fall for a man like Colt. He's too hard-hearted. I think someone must have hurt him once, someone he trusted. Of course, if he only sees women like Marsha, he deserves what he gets."

"You are in love," Carmen concluded.

"Of course I love him. He's been part of my life since I was five years old."

"No, in love."

Belle met her friend's wise gaze and sympathetic smile with a stoic shrug. The heart had its own confidante. Colt had always been hers.

Carmen patted her hand. "There," she soothed. "Don't fret about it. Things have a way of working out."

"So why are you worried about Leah and Darrel?"

Carmen sighed. "I wish I knew what was going on."

Colt left his office and stopped by the desk. The air seemed thicker, more potent than the heaviness just before a storm. Belle held her breath for a few seconds, then let it out slowly and carefully. When his eyes met hers, she was composed.

He spoke to Carmen. "I'll be out for the rest of

the day. Slocum and I will be touring the facilities of the supply company.''

That reminded her of something she'd thought of while talking to Mary the other day. "Oh, Colt, I just had an idea…uh, that's okay. On second thought, it's probably not a good one." She donned a bright smile to waylay questions.

He watched her without speaking for an eternity, a darkness in his eyes that she couldn't fathom. Colt was troubled about something. Her heart gave a pang.

"It might be late when I get home," he said to her.

"You won't be in for dinner?"

"No." He walked out without another word. The tension in the room eased considerably.

"Well, well, well," Carmen said. "Isn't he in a snit about something?" It wasn't really a question. Her eyes sparkled behind her bifocals.

Belle was at once worried about him. "What do you think is wrong?"

Carmen shrugged. "Time will tell, I think. Okay, Pierre says he will have the cake ready. The dress is hemmed. Colt and Slocum and Slocum's brother have tuxes. Darrel and Jamie have each rented one."

As they went over their checklist for the wedding, which seemed to be hurtling toward them like a freight train on a downhill track, Belle again had the feeling of time passing, of missing out on life's important things. She was pensive the rest of the day. The office seemed dull without Colt's dynamic presence.

At four forty-five, she received a call from a sales representative, which kept her tied up until after six. She was the last one out of the office.

Once she was on the street, restlessness seized her. She moseyed along the busy avenue while others rushed. She gazed into store windows and finally stopped for a slice of pizza for dinner. She sat on a high stool to eat, then left the tiny shop and meandered toward the condo. It would take thirty minutes at a brisk walk.

About halfway home, she decided to cut across a small park. Although it was after seven, there was plenty of daylight. It would be safe enough. She flipped her purse strap over her head so that no one could grab it from her shoulder and make off with her money and credit card.

She stopped and looked at a flower bed filled with summer blossoms. It was so lovely, it made her heart ache.

The sadness inherent in great beauty overcame her—the intensity of it, the wild fling of color and grace, the fragility. The brevity. A season and, *poof,* it was gone. Each one deserved an ode—

Tears filled her eyes.

Impatient with herself, she wiped them away. Now she was crying over flowers, for heaven's sake. She had to get over this…this…this yearning and the love that had no place to go.

She rocked back on her heels and considered the future. Everyone had lessons to learn in life. She knew it was futile to wish for the impossible. She had done that at her mother's death, at being sent off to boarding school, at times when her father had forgotten her. She rose and trudged on, entering a small grove of oak trees.

The path she followed through the park circled a

play area. Off to one side was a gazebo, one of the old-fashioned kind where bands could play in summer. She wondered if any ever did. She paused to study the ornate folly.

A couple had stopped on the other side of the white structure. Through the lacy gingerbread trim, she could see them, the man bent toward the woman, her staring at the ground, head down as if shy...or being scolded.

Belle realized the man's posture was stiff and angry. With a gasp, she recognized him.

Darrel. Leah's fiancé.

Carmen was right. He was seeing another woman. Belle gasped when he handed the woman a small wad of money.

Blackmail!

Belle clasped her hands at her breasts. That was the only explanation. The woman had some hold over Darrel. He was trapped by his love for Leah and wanted to protect her from whatever this horrible woman had on him....

No, no. Get a grip. It could be something quite simple. The woman had loaned him money and he was paying her back.

No.

She'd done some work for the accounting firm—
No.

Belle tried to think of a plausible reason for Darrel to be giving money to some strange woman in a park tucked away in a quiet square in the city. Nothing.

Darrel waved his arm in a furious gesture. The woman raised her head defiantly. Belle saw that she was older than Darrel, quite a bit older. More confused, Belle hesitated before rushing into the fray and demanding an introduction to the woman.

When the CPA stalked off in one direction and the woman wandered on down the park path, Belle was uncertain who to follow. She decided on the woman.

At ten, Belle heard Colt's key in the lock. Weariness showed in the slope of his shoulders, in the way he held his jacket, flung over his shoulder and supported by one finger.

She decided not to blurt out her news until he had a few moments to relax. "How was the meeting with Mr. Walters? I thought the sale was complete."

"It is. The problem is I don't have a manager for the new division. Henry basically ran that part of the business through his assistant or his sons."

"Why don't you hire Slocum to run it? He's been working there all his life. He and his brother probably know more than Mr. Walters."

Colt stopped in the act of pulling off his tie. He gave her a narrow-eyed scrutiny as if suspecting her of ulterior motives in the suggestion.

"Slocum, huh?" Colt tossed his jacket and tie on a chair, kicked off his shoes, unbuttoned his collar and rolled his cuffs back.

Belle was delighted he appeared to be considering it. "He interviewed for a position with a law firm yesterday. You'd better snap him up before he accepts."

"He's leaving his father's office?"

She nodded and went to hang up his suit jacket in the closet. Before she could complete the act, he took the coat from her hands.

"You're not here to pick up after me," he told her in a near snarl. "I'm a big boy. I take care of my own things."

"Well, excuse me," she snapped right back, fed up with his attitude toward her, which had been wary, sardonic or hateful all week, according to his mood at the moment.

She had tried to be considerate of him, especially when she was dying to tell him of her findings on Darrel and the strange woman. She reined in her tongue. "Would you like a piece of carrot cake? I brought some home from the deli."

He sighed and draped the jacket on a hanger. He looped the tie over the coat and stored them in the hall closet.

"I'm sorry for being a grouch. It's been a hard day. A hard week. Month," he finally settled on. His mouth quirked in one of his cynical smiles.

"Because of me?"

He hesitated in the hall. "Because of what's between us. We're both normal specimens of the human race. Proximity adds its own problems."

"I've wanted you a lot longer than a month," she said softly, the terrible sadness rolling over her. "The wanting isn't the problem. It's what goes with it. I think you're afraid to let anyone get beyond your carefully drawn boundaries. They might get too close...and find the real Colt McKinnon."

He stuck a hand on his hip. "Don't hit me with pop psychobabble. I'm not in the mood."

She ignored the storm warnings and crossed the room. "Is he such a bad guy?" She laid a hand over his heart. "Doesn't his heart beat with hope and despair and longings just like any other?"

He removed her hand.

She touched his cheek, the yearning rising sharp and urgent in her. "The man I know would give his life to spare a friend any hurt. The man I once knew held me when grief was unbearable and shared my tears. He cheered me up when I was homesick. He chased away the demons. He listened to my dreams without once laughing. Is he really such a bad guy?"

Taking her wrists, he held her away from him, but she could feel his heat pouring over her, soothing and exciting at the same time. The certainty of her love for him rose in her. And the certainty of his rejection. He didn't speak but merely gazed at her, his face cast in stone.

"All right," she said in agreement to his silent demand to be left alone.

He dropped her wrists and stepped back. "Don't push so hard, kiddo. Someday some man will think you're the greatest thing since chocolate and sweep you off your feet. Be a little patient."

With that homily, he sauntered off down the hall toward his bedroom.

"Be careful what you predict. Someday you might have to eat those words," she called out.

He paused. "Chocolate is one of my favorite foods." His eyes swept over her. Then he went into his bedroom and closed the door, the sardonic chuckle lingering behind him.

Belle leaned against the wall, weak-kneed and more confused than ever by his attitude. Did he want her...or did he not?

"That is the question," she declaimed aloud, borrowing a line from Shakespeare. "Whether 'tis nobler to endure the slings and arrows of outrageous fortune, or Colt McKinnon," she said loudly, passing his door on the way to her room.

After the previous night's contretemps, Belle decided not to include Colt in her weekend plans. She dressed in jeans, jogging shoes and a chambray shirt. Tucking her hair on top of her head, she added a baseball cap, the brim low over her eyes to disguise her face. After a quick breakfast, she left a note on the refrigerator and headed out.

In ten minutes, she was at the park. She stopped to admire a flowering bush near the bandstand. Her quarry was nowhere in sight. At noon, she was ready to call it a bust. She'd wandered around the small park, keeping an eye on the gazebo, while she inspected flowers and rocks, trees and everything else in the place.

Just as she was giving up, the woman appeared.

Or perhaps *emerged* was the better term. Apparently the woman Darrel was seeing lived under the gazebo. Yesterday, after a careful look all around, the woman had pulled aside a loose piece of latticework and disappeared underneath.

The hair stood up on Belle's neck. This was really bizarre. She followed at a discreet distance.

The woman went around to all the trash cans in the area and collected cans and bottles. She put these in a bag she withdrew from her coat pocket, then she went into a deli and ordered lunch.

Her clothing was another odd thing, Belle thought.

She was dressed in slacks and a shirt with a long black raincoat over them. The air was eighty-five degrees.

Belle bought a candy bar at a market across the street and returned to her vigil. For the rest of the day, she followed the woman around from trash can to trash can, then back to the gazebo. The woman pulled out a bag of cans and struggled to her feet, then tried to lift the bag.

Belle rushed forward. "Here, let me help you." She took part of the weight. "Where are you going?"

The woman gave her a suspicious once-over. "None of your business. Let go of my cans, or I'll yell. I have friends, you know."

Belle was pretty sure the woman was bluffing. "I'm Belle. I'm...uh...Darrel is a friend of mine." She held her breath to see if she would be accepted or if this would set the other female off. The bag lady and Darrel hadn't parted on the best of terms.

"Darrel?"

"Uh-huh. You were talking to him yesterday, remember?"

"Of course I do. I'm not crazy." she let go the sack and gestured impatiently. "Well, come along. The center doesn't stay open all night."

Belle slung the pack over her back. She felt like a peddler as people on the street glanced at her in amusement. The woman led the way to a recycling center.

A woman there knew Belle's companion. "Pat, how's it going? That's quite a load. Who's your friend?"

"Not a friend of mine. My son sent her. She's probably from city services."

The bag slipped from Belle's hands. She gaped at Darrel's mother. "No, I'm not. Really. I just happened by. I've seen you with Darrel once before. You're his mother?"

"Yes."

The recycling woman weighed the cans and counted out a small number of bills and some change. She handed it to Pat.

"Thanks, Julie, I'll see you next month." Pat took off briskly down the street in the direction of the park.

Belle tagged along. "Mrs. Henderson—"

"I suppose Darrel wants you to talk me into moving in with him. I'm not going to. I won't be dependent on my son or anyone for a home."

"So you sell cans and bottles for a living?" Belle fell into step beside the older woman.

"I used to be a blueprint clerk, but the company downsized and I was let go. That was nineteen months ago. No one wants a fifty-three-year-old woman with no skills. I lost my apartment, but I won't take charity. My husband is dead, but I get a pension, so I'm not destitute."

"I see," Belle said sympathetically. "So...do you live under the gazebo?"

"Yes. It's a snug place."

Belle nodded. She was beginning to comprehend several things. When they arrived at the park, she was so deep in thought, she didn't see Darrel until it was too late for her to hide. She smiled brightly at him.

"Your mom and I have had a busy day," she said.

His face flushed. "She's not crazy. It's a sort of

neurosis, the doctors say. She and my grandmother had to live with my grandmother's parents for a while. They made their life miserable, so she won't live with anyone, including me.''

"I understand," Belle said gently. "When are you going to introduce your mother to Leah?"

"Who's Leah?" Pat asked.

Belle realized Pat's eyes were the same light blue as Darrel's and their lips were the same shape. Mother and son. She was relieved for Carmen's and Leah's sakes.

"My fiancée," he said when Belle didn't answer.

Pat beamed. "It's about time you married. I want a dozen grandkids."

Darrel ignored the remark. "Mom, you haven't been to my place all week."

"I was busy," she said vaguely. "I spent the night of the storm over at Ida's house. She works at the center."

Darrel shifted restlessly. He looked miserable. Belle tried to catch his eye, but he refused to look at her.

"I have an idea," she said. It came to her in a flash. "Dee and Kelley need a receptionist to handle the phone and assign the maids to the places to be cleaned. They're working out of Kelley's apartment and using her answering machine. Pat could take over the scheduling for them and maybe fill in when they need a maid." She looked a question at Pat.

"Sure. I'm not too proud to do housework."

Belle and Pat looked at Darrel.

He flushed again. "It's fine with me. But you can't continue to live under a bandstand."

"She'll be able to afford her own place after she starts work. Meanwhile, you'll need a phone. Why don't you think about staying at Darrel's until you save enough for the deposit on an apartment?"

"I suppose I can do that. But only for a little while."

Darrel shook his head. "It can't be this simple. I've been arguing with her for months—"

"It's different when you're pulling your own weight," Belle broke in. "Pat, why don't I introduce you to Kelley and Dee of the Mighty Maids service? I'll invite them to dinner tomorrow night. Can you come? You and Leah, too, Darrel."

Belle quickly arranged the meeting and talked Pat into going home with Darrel. On her way to the penthouse, she decided if the maid service didn't work out, then she would just have to talk Colt into hiring Pat. The receptionist was pregnant and would be leaving in three months anyway.

When she arrived at the penthouse, she rushed into to tell Colt the news. The place was empty. A note on the refrigerator said he'd gone to the ranch.

Without inviting her.

It hurt more than she cared to admit. So maybe he needed some time apart to come to grips with the attraction between them. Or maybe he merely didn't want to be around her any more than necessary.

Colt rode until he was exhausted, then he rubbed down the gelding and fed it a bucket of oats. The ranch house was dark when he went inside. He'd forgotten to leave on a light when he'd left, heading across the rolling pasture and up along the limestone

outcropping as if all hell were chasing him instead of
his own conscience.

The problem came back to the same thing. Belle.

He showered, dressed and headed for the small
town a few miles down the road. The bar located on
a corner across from the tiny post office blasted coun-
try-western music and laughter when he parked out
front. He went in.

The lights were appropriately dim. The music had
softened to a slow number. The bar stools were padded. He selected one in the corner, well away from
two cowboys who talked over a couple of cold beers.

After chugging one beer and ordering another, he
turned to watch the few couples who circled around
the dance area, their arms wrapped around each other
as if they might be blown away at any moment.

He grimaced. His disposition was sour tonight.

Three women came in. They spotted the two cowboys and joined them at the bar, two gals on one side
and one on the other of the men. That left one woman
as odd man out.

Her eyes met Colt's. She smiled.

He nodded and turned back to contemplating the
suds clinging to the glass as he sipped the brew.

Another ten minutes went by.

"Hi," a voice said at his shoulder. "You look
lonely, cowboy."

Colt swiveled to the woman. From down the bar,
the other four watched, grins on their faces. He knew
they'd put her up to approaching him.

He pasted a smile on his face. "That's right."

"So am I." She slid onto the stool next to him.
"Maybe if we join up, we can chase it away."

"Sure. You want something to drink?"

"A soda would be nice. I'm not much for beer."

"There's wine. Or champagne."

Her eyes brightened. "Champagne, please. I'm Sue."

"Colt."

She laughed and did flirty things with her eyes. "We had already figured that out. There aren't many new faces around here."

"Why don't your friends join us at a table?" He picked up his beer and called out her order to the bartender.

The night passed pleasantly enough. At two, when the place blinked its lights, signaling it was time to close, Colt saw Sue and her girlfriends glance at each other. He knew they expected him to take her home.

He thought about it for all of two seconds. "Well, that was fun. I 'spect we'll see each other again sometime seeing that we're neighbors. Thanks for taking a lonely cowpoke in," he said directly to Sue, touching her lightly on the shoulder. He waved to the others and headed for the door.

In his car, he wondered why he hadn't followed up on the invitation in her eyes. That's why he'd taken up her offer to join him.

Again the house was dark when he got home. He found his way through the utility room by feel and fumbled for a light on the kitchen wall. When it came on, he stared at the empty room as if he'd never seen it.

It had been a mistake to have Belle out there. Now she haunted him at the ranch as well as at the condo. She added light and cheer to any room. She had the knack of making any place exclusively hers so that it was forever empty when she wasn't around.

He turned out the light and made his way in the dark to his room. He cursed while he undressed. Falling into bed, he determined not to dream of anything…especially Belle.

But he knew he would. And he did.

An hour later he rose and dressed and headed for the city.

Chapter Eight

The condo was softly lit when Colt entered around midnight. Low voices wafted from the television where a movie was in progress. A vase of roses added fragrance and beauty to the coffee table. The pot of ivy was on a cabinet. One slender foot protruded from the arm of the sofa.

He walked into the room and looked down at Belle, fast asleep on the sofa. A colorful afghan was partly draped over her, partly fallen on the floor. Her hair clung like silk threads to a cushion. One arm curled around her head, the other lay across her tummy. She wore a golden yellow knit outfit. Some kind of pajama, he assumed.

Going to his bedroom, he changed to jogging shorts and a T-shirt, then went into the kitchen to find something to eat. He hadn't had supper.

Belle came in while he was fixing a ham sandwich. "There's homemade chicken gumbo in the fridge."

"This will do."

She heated a bowl of gumbo in the microwave oven and took a seat at the table. He stood by the counter and finished the sandwich, then washed it down with a soda. He scrutinized Belle while she rinsed her bowl and put it in the dishwasher.

"I had Carmen and Leah over for dinner," she said. "Darrel came. So did his mother."

She leaned her hip against the counter. The golden material looked soft. Touchable. Colt realized she was waiting for him to say something.

"So you got them all set up for their big day?" He heard the sarcastic edge to his tone and winced.

Belle didn't seem to notice. "I think so. Would you believe Darrel's mom was a bag lady, and she was the woman he was meeting? He thought Leah and Carmen would think his family crazy if they heard about his mother."

Colt listened while she explained the situation. He was incredulous. "You hung around a city park, then followed some strange woman—"

"Darrel's mother."

"You didn't know that." He huffed out an angry breath and tried for control. It didn't work. "Don't you have any sense? What if she'd been a real nutcase, a serial killer or a drug runner?"

"She wasn't like that. She was neat and clean and very industrious—"

He threw up his hands. "I should have taken you to the ranch. That's the only way I can keep an eye on you."

"Why didn't you?" Her quiet tone penetrated his anger.

The atmosphere thickened noticeably. He studied her for a long ten seconds. "I needed some time alone. I wanted to pick up a woman."

She flushed, then paled, but she didn't flinch. "Did you find someone?"

"Yes."

"Did you take her to the ranch?"

"I thought of it." He continued to hold her gaze for another minute, then he rinsed his glass and put it away. When he turned, Belle had moved over to the door. She'd put the length of the kitchen between them, he realized.

"About Darrel's mom," she said as if there had been no break in the earlier conversation. "I wondered if maybe Pat could take the receptionist's place when she goes out on maternity leave. Dee will leave her day job around then and handle the business. Kelley plans to keep working as a personal shopper while they grow their client base."

He noticed how rosy her lips looked next to the strained paleness of her face. She studied the plants at the window and refused to look at him. He couldn't read a thing from her expression.

The old Belle would have been in tears if her feelings were hurt. This new Belle, she was a different person altogether, with nuances rather than blatant emotion.

"So what do you think about Darrel's mom working in the office? She's had experience, and she's very nice looking."

"She can put in an application. Tell Carmen to set up an interview."

"I will. Thank you," the new, quiet Belle said.

"Carmen is ecstatic about Pat. It must be hard to be a parent and worry that your child is making a mistake."

"You should try being a guardian sometime. It's worse." The cynical quip popped out unbidden.

A slight flush put color in her cheeks again. "In three more months, your ordeal will be over."

"If I turn over the trust fund."

She tilted her head to one side as if listening to some melody only she could hear. "You will. Or else I'll call for an audit and take you to court if one penny is missing or mismanaged."

He froze in place. Belle...*Belle*...had actually threatened him. He unstuck his shocked muscles and paced the kitchen. His fury mounted with each step.

"I've worked my buns off for years so that Hal could play poker with his cronies, so that you could attend the best schools in the States and take vacations all over the world. I studied markets and learned more than I ever wanted to know about bonds and securities, just so you could have an easy life."

Not only that, but he'd learned about Shakespeare and Milton and dozens of other writers and poets so he could keep up with Belle and talk to her about her studies.

"This is the thanks I get? A threat? As soon as you're twenty-one, you can take the damn money and handle it yourself." His grin was cruel. "You probably think a debenture is a set of false teeth."

"It's a promissory note," she said with grave dignity, and walked out, her head high.

Hell, he ought to let some fortune hunter marry her

and lose her whole wad. He stalked down the hall, too mad to think about sleep.

Belle made it to her room...the guest room, she reminded herself savagely. Her throat cramped with pent feelings, with the hot, wild tears that wanted to pour out of her, with all the misery of the past eight years while being shipped from pillar to post, of having no place and no one of her own. Colt had made it quite clear with his pick-up date and snide remark that he wished he didn't have to put up with her.

She sat on the bed and hugged a pillow and stared into the dark...and stared...and stared....

Her face was all hot and achy. The inside of her nose felt swollen. Her whole head felt as if it would explode. She stared into the darkness and swallowed again and again.

All the bright promise of life, all the bright hope she'd harbored when she'd arrived, were muted by the gloom. The darkness reached all the way inside, to the farthest corners of her being, and all the light was gone.

The door banged open and flew back on its hinges. The light snapped on. She blinked as it hurt her eyes.

Colt stopped inside her room. He looked furiously angry. She didn't care. At that moment, he could have pointed a gun at her and she wouldn't have ducked. At that moment in time, it was beyond her to care.

His expression was hard. "Don't," he said in a snarl.

She stared at him and wished for the darkness. It was easier to face than Colt McKinnon.

Her guardian. Her protector. Her nemesis.

The irony of it was awful, a truth that lodged in her throat and choked the tears that wanted to fall. She would rather die than cry in front of him. Or admit her love, her hopes, her dreams. She at last understood how very foolish it had been to come to him.

The churn of emotion brought out a fine sweat all over her. She swallowed and held on. She knew about holding on, from one Sunday to the next, waiting for Colt's call, for her father to remember to let her come home, for life to be sweet again.

He came toward her, sat beside her on the bed. "Don't," he said again, softer but still tinged with cruelty.

Words crowded and bunched, joined the ache in her chest. She didn't say them. She had nothing left to say.

When he touched her face, she didn't move. His hand felt cool against her hot skin. He sighed. "Don't cry."

"I'm not." She got the words out, then clamped all the rest of them inside, refusing to speak.

"I was angry. When you threatened me, I saw red." He went into the bathroom and returned with a damp washcloth. He rubbed it over her eyes and cheeks.

She saw her face in the mirror. It was splotched with red and white as if she had a rash that chose random spots to appear. Her eyes seemed too big.

"Lie down," Colt advised. He stood and pulled the covers aside.

She sat there hugging the pillow and wouldn't, couldn't look at him.

"Belle, I'm sorry. I didn't mean to hurt you—"

She couldn't let that pass. "Yes, you did."

He ran a hand over his face. "Okay, I did. You made me angry with that threat. I've never taken a penny of your money. I should hope you know that."

"Yes, I do. I said it because…"

"Because?"

Because I can't bear it that you went to another woman. She couldn't say that. She had no rights over him. No woman did. He would marry for connections.

She sighed, her dreams too tarnished to keep, too precious to toss away like a used receipt. "Let's let it go. We're both tired and saying things we'll regret."

He touched her shoulder, then urged her onto the bed. She lay down and let him cover her with the sheet. When he bent to her, she let him kiss her, a gentle kiss at odds with their grim faces.

There was no smile in her as she watched him frown and ran a hand through his hair. He bent suddenly and crushed her mouth under his as if dissatisfied with the first kiss.

Then, somehow, his hand was fisted in her hair. The kiss went deep. She felt his demand for a response and the urging of his mouth against hers. His tongue stroked her lips, asking for entrance.

She sighed and opened to him. And somehow her arms were wrapped around him, her hands entangled in his hair.

He dropped to the bed and stretched his sinewy length over hers, the sheet bunching between them. The residue of their anger survived the kiss and became embedded in it. The gentleness, what there had been of it, was gone, and now there was only harsh desire.

They slipped past the point of denial and claimed each other with a hunger that refused to recognize the boundaries he had set. She was filled with blinding joy...and blazing anger that he still wouldn't see all the things that were possible for them....

"We're not going below the waist," he said hoarsely, adamantly. He stripped her top over her head and threw his T-shirt aside.

His hot chest seared into her breasts. She gasped and couldn't breathe, then she did in deep, hard draughts that made her shake.

"The hunger is so terrible, a monster gnawing at my insides," she tried to explain.

"Don't you think I know that?" He bit her shoulder, along her arm, then licked all the spots that burned and ached, not with pain, but with need. He kissed her mouth, her ear, her neck, her breasts.

She stroked his back, then slipped her hands inside his waistband and caressed his rock-hard buttocks. When she drew a finger along the narrow crevice, he bucked against her, then held very still. He didn't tell her to stop.

"This can't go on," he told her, moving his torso against hers, delighting her.

"Why?"

"Because."

"I know. I don't have connections."

He raised up and looked at her in the soft lamp-light. "Connections?"

"Like Marsha, or someone like her."

"Belle," he said, exasperation in his tone. "You

have all the connections you'll ever need. You have
me and all Gulfco behind you. You're the match for
any man in the state. You got that?''

Anyone but you. ''Yes, I got it.'' She stroked her
fingers up his spine to his neck, then raked them
through his hair, loving its thickness, the silken black-
ness against her skin, the warmth she found. ''Kiss
me again.''

''I must be crazy,'' he complained on a half groan.

But he did it. They kissed for hours, until her lips
were red and sensitive, until he had little bruises
where she couldn't help but suck his skin in passion
unchained.

It was all so incredibly wonderful.

''Rest,'' he finally ordered, moving to the side of
her.

She wondered if she dared go to sleep. No dream
had ever been this good. She sighed and snuggled
against his shoulder. He held her, his arms a loose
circle around her shoulders and across her waist. The
last thing she heard was the beating of his heart.

Belle woke with a start. The warmth cupped around
her back moved away, leaving her chilled. She rolled
over and watched as Colt sat up on the side of the
bed.

''I can't believe I slept here,'' he muttered. The
anger was overridden by a weariness reflected in his
face.

''Not like sleeping with the woman you picked up,
you mean?'' she asked, lifting one eyebrow. ''Or
didn't you go below the waist with her, either?''

He pushed himself upright. ''I didn't know you had

a tongue with a razor edge on it. This is a whole new side I haven't seen—Belle, the shrew.''

"We all have hidden facets." She leveled a stare at him. "You have your share of secret vices."

"Jealousy isn't a virtue, either."

She didn't flinch. "Yes, I'm jealous of the woman you picked up. What did she have to offer that I haven't?"

He went into the bathroom and splashed water over his face. Drying off, he came back into the bedroom. Belle propped herself against the pillows. A terrible calm had come over her, like that in the center of a hurricane.

"No complications." He walked to the door. "No guilt. No strings. No repercussions."

"Have I asked for anything?" she challenged. "Have I demanded your undying devotion? Have I indicated I expect more than the passion of the moment?"

He faced her. "You're ready to fall in love," he said, obviously tired of the argument. "I don't want to be involved in your fairy tale, nor the acrimony that will surely follow when you wake and find your dream prince is a frog, after all."

She raised her knees under the sheet and crossed her arms over them. "What are you talking about?"

"Life. It's real, kiddo."

"I have never mistaken fantasy for reality. You and Dad struck oil. That was real. My mother died. That was real. So did my father. Another reality bite. You're attracted, but you don't want to become involved with me. Why? What are you afraid of? What is reality for you? What is fantasy?"

"It's a fantasy to think we can become lovers and continue as business partners. It would lead to—"

"Complications. And you don't want any." She studied him, trying to see inside and understand what he wanted. "Wouldn't there have been any complications with Marsha?"

"No."

"Why?"

Colt banged the heel of his fist on the door facing. "Because there was no emotion involved." He cast Belle a harsh glance. "Emotion messes up things, keeps a person from seeing life as it really is."

Her slow smile was mysterious, mocking. Belle, the wise woman, gazed at him from her amber eyes. "Or it colors everything a delightful rosy hue and makes the bad seem better, or at least bearable."

"Ever the optimist."

"You used to be the same. Why else would you and Dad sink all your money into drilling for oil?"

"That was a calculated risk. We knew what we were doing." He tossed her a "beat that" challenge.

"So do I," she said, her voice as low as a whisper of song on a morning breeze, almost a croon.

For a moment he almost believed her. Until the sun shining through a slit in the curtain hit her hair and brightened the light brown to golden red tones, reminding him of the fire that lived in her slender, vibrant body.

"You think you want me. What you really want to know is how everything works between a man and woman. I'm not going to teach you."

"Someone will."

He didn't rise to the blatant challenge. Turning, he

headed out the door, then stopped and glanced over his shoulder at her. "I had always slept alone until I slept with you."

She blinked, then nodded solemnly as if they'd made a pact. "Good."

He scowled the whole time—during the shower and while he dressed for work. He'd all but admitted he couldn't go to another woman.

When she walked into the kitchen wearing a peach blouse and a white skirt, he glared at her. She ignored him.

He carefully stepped around her while he toasted a bagel and hunted for the jelly, but he bumped into her in front of the fridge where she was getting milk for a bowl of cereal.

Her breast brushed his arm when she reached past him for the coffeepot. Every hair on his body stood up. His hip touched hers when he dropped the jelly spoon into the dishwasher. His knees hit hers when he sat at the table.

The roomy kitchen suddenly seemed too small to hold them. He moved his legs to the side. In total silence they drank their juice, ate their meal and shared the morning paper over coffee. Their fingers touched when they reached for the comics at the same time.

She lifted her hands, palms out as if signaling surrender, and let him take the pages. She picked up the home feature section and read about decorating a den.

Finally she set the paper aside. "Perhaps it's because of the wedding today."

"What?" he snapped.

"Us. Whatever is happening between us right now.

It's never been this way. Maybe we've outgrown our need for each other.'' She paused, then sighed heavily. ''Like families that grow apart and never see each other.''

''Maybe.'' He got up and refilled his cup. ''I've got some work to do. What are your plans?''

''I'm going over to help Mary dress. I'll take my things. I'll see you at the ceremony.''

He nodded and disappeared. She finished the paper, then showered and manicured her nails while heated rollers added controlled waves to her hair. ''I'm gone,'' she called at the door of the study.

''You need me to drive you?'' he called back.

''No. I have a cab on the way.''

On the way to Mary's apartment, which would soon be home to the bridal pair, Belle tried to figure out the strange situation between her and Colt. She had no past experiences to compare with it. Odder still, she felt all weepy now whereas earlier she'd been as angry as Colt. It was just too much to figure out.

At Mary's place, all was chaos. About fifty relatives were crowded inside, the guys switching between baseball and the preseason football games, the women setting out food or putting it away. Mary's bedroom door was closed.

''See if she'll open it to you,'' her mother invited. ''She said she didn't want to see anyone.''

Belle knocked and called out Mary's name. ''Shall I come in, or do you need to be alone?''

The door opened, and Mary pulled her inside. She locked the door behind them. ''Tell me I'm doing the right thing.''

"You're doing the right thing." Belle placed her dress and case on a chair.

"You don't think I'm ruining his life? Slocum is so wonderful. He could have anyone...some debutante—"

"He loves you," Belle said firmly. "He's an adult. Let him make up his own mind."

"I'm so afraid. I've made one mistake. I don't want to make another and drag him into it. His father still hasn't forgiven us, but he's coming to the wedding."

"Do you want to have Slocum's child?"

"Well, yes, I would love to have children." Mary gave her a puzzled glance.

"Mr. Walters will come around when he sees his first grandchild. Neither son has given him grandchildren. I think he's getting worried about that."

"Then we'll have one right away. I wasn't sure—" Mary broke off and stared at Belle. "I think I'm going crazy, thinking about having children when I haven't got through the marriage ceremony yet. I'm so nervous."

"I'm sure Slocum is, too."

But he wasn't. When the wedding started, Slocum turned and waited for his bride to come to him, his stance relaxed, his face wreathed in a smile that made Belle's heart ache, it was so beautiful and tender.

After the couple said their vows, she noticed that Mr. Walters swiped at his eyes and nose a couple of times when he thought no one was looking.

The reception at the country club was everything a bride could wish for—flowers, music, food, the most perfect wedding cake Belle had ever seen. Colt had taken care of the room and the music; Slocum and

Mary the rest. Belle had handled the delicate maneuvering between the two men and their pride and had arranged everything with Mary.

Slocum's older brother, the best man, gave a long and glowing toast. Colt surprised them by adding his own toast, mixed with a little ribald humor and an account of the near fight at the ranch that had everyone howling with laughter.

"Sorry, old man," he said in apology to the groom, "I've only had one female to take care of, and she came just about grown-up, so I didn't get a chance to grow into the parental role."

"Maybe you'll get that chance," Kelley called, a wicked gleam in her eye. "Maybe you'll be next at the altar."

Colt's eyes met Belle's. "I've avoided that noose for years. I think I'll hold out a while longer."

But when Slocum flipped his bride's garter behind him into the crowd, it went straight to Colt. There was laughter and teasing. He took it with a good-humored smile.

Belle danced with Slocum, then Mary's father, then Mr. Walters. She liked him even if he was something of a curmudgeon with his sons. "Have you met my boy Harry?" he asked, whirling them around the floor like a dervish.

"Yes."

"What'd you think of him?"

"He's big, like his dad." She grinned up at the friendly giant.

"All muscle," he said proudly. "Here, Harry, take this woman off my hands. I'm about to make myself dizzy with all this twirling about."

Belle landed in Harry's arms while his dad went to the bar and ordered a beer. "You're the MBA brother, right?" She'd spoken only briefly to him during the rehearsal and at the dinner afterward earlier in the week.

"That's right. I'm supposed to run the business while Slocum is groomed to run for the legislature."

"I don't think that plan is going to work out. Slocum will be starting to work for Gulfco when he returns from his honeymoon." Belle was glad to find Harry didn't think dancing was some kind of race.

As the reception wore on, she found Harry at her side more and more. They ate supper together on a quiet veranda and watched the sun begin to set.

"Autumn will be here before we know it," Harry remarked, a bit of nostalgia in the words.

"Yes. I suppose I should think of going back to school. I have another year."

"What are you studying?"

"Business, but I'm thinking of switching to psychology. I think I like people better than numbers."

"You should go into something you like," he advised. "The rest of your life is a long time to be miserable."

Colt joined them when they went back inside. "Dance?" he asked Belle.

She hesitated, then nodded. He led her to the floor.

A dark emotion flicked through his eyes. "Did you have to think about it first?"

"Yes. I thought it might be better if we avoided each other until...for a while."

"Until I can control my mad lust?" he suggested, his tone harsh.

"Well, until I can control mine." She ignored the fluttering of her pulses and tried for calm. When she glanced at him, she found his gaze poring over her. If a person could be consumed in a glance, this would do it, she thought, dazed by the flames, then the heat when he drew her close, then closer.

"You smell good enough to eat," he muttered. "I thought Slocum's brother was going to take a bite out of you out there on the patio."

"He was being nice."

"You like him?"

"Yes."

"Huh."

"Huh, what?"

"Nothing."

"What's wrong with Harry?"

"Nothing." Colt glared down at her. "He's too old for you. He's at least thirty-five."

"You're thirty-four."

"Yeah. I'm too old, too. You can do better."

"Than Harry? Or you?"

"Either of us."

She stopped dancing. When she tried to draw away from him, he wouldn't let her go. After a brief and silent struggle, she gave in and let him guide her into a dim corner. She could feel every move of his thighs against hers through the long pink silk dress.

For a long magic moment, she pictured them as the bride and groom on the cake, dancing around and around under a bower of white roses, enchantment in the air.

Looking into Colt's stern gaze, she sighed. That, indeed, was fantasy.

Chapter Nine

"What was happening between you and Colt when you were dancing in that corner?" Kelley demanded at lunch. It was Thursday, almost two weeks after the wedding and the first time they had been able to get together.

"Just the usual—he's protecting me from this mad passion we have for each other while deflecting other men he doesn't consider suitable husband material."

Leah, who had joined them for the meal, stared at Belle, not sure which part of her statement to believe.

Kelley whooped with laughter. "You're supposed to warn us when you're going to do that, as in, Warning—Explosive Announcement Coming Up, remember?"

Belle smiled and shrugged philosophically. "I'll try."

She was filling in for Carmen who was on vacation that week. Pat, the former bag lady, was filling in for the receptionist, who was out again, and also taking calls for the Mighty Maids.

In the eleven days since the wedding, Belle had rarely seen Colt. He was working over at the new supply company every day. Slocum had taken over as vice president and general manager of the new division that would combine the pipeline supply company with the oil field supply one.

"Guess what?" Leah said with a shy smile.

Belle and Kelly looked at her expectantly.

"Darrel and I have set the date. We're going to have the wedding over Thanksgiving weekend. My dad will come up for it. My brothers and their families will be here. Plus Darrel's mom. Do you two think you could come? It'll be small, but I'd like to have you. Also Colt and Jamie, and Mary and Slocum, of course."

"Wild horses wouldn't keep me away," Belle assured the other young woman, who was nearly two years older than herself, but seemed younger for some reason.

"Me, either," Kelley agreed. "Jamie and I have decided to give our fathers until Christmas to accept our seeing each other, then we're going to announce our engagement. We're thinking of a Valentine's Day wedding."

"That's good. By marrying next year, you'll get a tax break this year since you'll still be able to file single returns," Belle told Kelley.

Kelley studied Belle for a long moment, then smiled and touched her hand. "Thank you. I'll remind Jamie of that."

For the rest of the meal, they discussed weddings.

Like Leah, Kelley wanted something smaller than Mary and Slocum's nuptials. "Neither of us comes from a large family, so it shouldn't be a problem."

"Mine will be really tiny," Belle lamented, "just me, the way my life is shaping up."

"You'll meet your dream man," Leah assured her.

That night, alone in the penthouse, she prowled the television channels, unable to settle on a show. Colt had left a message for her. He would be in later that evening.

Just as she heard his key in the lock, the telephone rang, startling her. She took a deep breath and tried to release the tension coiling in her as Colt entered the condo. "Hello," she said into the receiver.

"Belle? This is Harry Walters."

"Harry. It's nice to hear from you." She smiled at Colt when he finally glanced her way. "How are you?"

"Fine." He hesitated. "I wondered if you'd like to go out to dinner Saturday night. There's a new Italian place that Slocum recommended the other day."

"Oh. Well." She wrapped her finger in the spiral cord while she tried to decide if this was a good idea.

Colt hung up his jacket. He stripped off his tie and disappeared down the hall.

"If you're busy…"

"No," she said. "I'm not. It sounds delightful. I'd love to go."

"Great."

They made arrangements for him to pick her up at seven. She heard Colt in the kitchen when she hung up. She joined him there. "That was Harry. We're going to dinner Saturday night, this new Italian place—''

''I thought we'd go to the ranch,'' Colt broke in.

Her heart jumped, then plummeted into place again. ''I don't think there's any need for me to go.''

He gave her a frowning glance over the open refrigerator door. ''There's an auction on Arabian yearlings we need to check out. I'm thinking we should start a bloodline of show horses.''

Belle propped her shoulder against the door frame and watched him fix a sandwich. She thought of the past and the times she'd asked her father to let her raise Arabians. He'd refused, then he'd sold the ranch after sending her off to boarding school. It had been a shock. She'd felt betrayed and abandoned. Except for Colt and his visits.

''I don't have a ranch,'' she said. ''You don't need me to help you select stock. Your foreman is the one for that.''

She watched his lithe, muscular body as he moved about the kitchen. He wore a pair of jeans, out at both knees, and a faded T-shirt. As usual, he was barefoot.

Colt had been the one to make her understand her father's grief and his way of coming to terms with it by leaving the place where they'd been happy with her mother. Colt had become the stable influence in her life for the past eight years. He was her best friend and confidante. The one person whose opinion she listened to. The one she trusted above all others. The one she loved more than she'd ever dreamed possible....

Wrapping her arms across her chest, she held in all the yearning that welled from that love. She could no longer throw herself into Colt's arms and expect that he would comfort her the way he'd done in the past. There were too many volatile feelings between them, now.

He chuckled. "Aren't you an excellent judge of horseflesh as well as character?"

His teasing only made the longing that much harder to bear. "Not me," she managed lightly. "I'll stay here and try the Italian place with Harry."

Colt brought his plate over to the table. He gave her an ominous frown. "I thought we'd already had a conversation about him."

She held his pointed stare. "You think he's too old for me. I don't."

"Belle—"

"What have you really got against him? Other than he might be interested in me as a person, which you seem to have trouble believing. Maybe not all men want only to make love with me, then move on."

She couldn't believe she'd said that, not to Colt. He looked so flummoxed, he apparently couldn't believe it, either. However, she didn't take it back.

He hesitated, then told her, "I want only what's best for you, Belle, nothing more, nothing less."

She sighed, then managed a wry laugh and took her seat at the table. "I've never thought you wanted the worst, but how do you know what's best for another person? Do you know my dreams, my...my heart's wishes?"

He took a drink of beer and set the can down. "I think I know what you think they are."

"You sound like my father used to when he lectured me about wanting to come home—as if I don't know my own mind, but you do. That's presumptuous and condescending.''

''I've never meant to be either of those with you,'' he answered her quietly.

She hated it that they seemed at odds over everything. Once she'd thought they were in perfect tune, like two strings on a guitar. "Sex ruins everything, doesn't it?'' she asked rhetorically, the sadness of their lost friendship overcoming other emotions. She still wanted that friendship, but he didn't. Colt didn't want anything from anyone.

''It's a complication we don't need, that's for sure.'' He sounded tired…resigned…defeated.

Her eyes met his. It was as if she'd dived into a dark pool of some translucent material, but she still couldn't reach all the way to the bottom of those depths. Sensing the futility of further conversation, she bade him good-night and went to her room.

Colt couldn't concentrate on the catalog. The horses, their bloodlines, their histories, all went right out of his head as soon as he read the words. He and the foreman had gone over the possible purchases earlier and decided on a starting price and a final amount they were willing to give for each horse. He tossed the brochure aside and wondered why he was thinking of buying the horses.

The answer came to him with crystal clarity. Because of Belle. It was something she'd once wanted.

He shook his head. He couldn't give her the dreams of her youth, and that was what he was trying to do. She was no longer that child who thought the world revolved around wide open spaces and a fast horse.

The news came on the television. He realized it was late and he should go to bed. Why? He wouldn't sleep. Not with Belle out with Slocum's brother.

He paced the room, then with an oath, turned off the TV, flicked out the lights and headed out. Harry wouldn't seduce Belle—maybe—but she was ready to fall in love. It had to be with the right guy, someone good enough for her, someone to share her dreams and goals, to give her the home and the babies she wanted—

Gritting his teeth, he forced that line of thought from his mind and headed back to town. He arrived just before midnight. A lamp was on in the living room. He could feel the emptiness of the apartment. Belle wasn't home yet.

He kicked off his shoes in his bedroom and changed to an old sweat suit. Going into his study, he pulled out the list of marriage candidates he'd made after Belle's arrival.

After marking through the names of the Neanderthals, as Belle called them, and Slocum's, he studied the three left. One had been in trouble for drugs as a teenager, he'd discovered. He crossed it off. Another had married and was already divorced. Scratch that one.

He added a new name, then wrote a summary of their qualifying characteristics. Wealth. Check. Old family. Check. Degree. One had an MBA, the other a BS in engineering. Check. Career. The MBA, like Harry, worked in the family business. The engineer was a consultant to a venture capitalist firm. Check. Reputation. Neither was a playboy, according to his sources. Neither had been married, so there was no divorce. They were mid to late twenties in age, ideal for Belle.

For a second, his gut clenched at the thought of another man showing Belle how good and uncomplicated sex could be between a man and a woman. Husband and wife, he corrected. He didn't want anyone touching Belle who hadn't committed one hundred percent to her.

Okay, either of these two would do. He'd arrange a meeting, maybe a dinner at the country club. Yeah, that should do it. Both the MBA and the engineer played golf. Belle was a decent hacker. He jotted a note to remind himself to take care of it first thing next week.

He flicked out the light and leaned his head against the leather executive chair. God, he was tired, more so than a coyote chasing a roadrunner. A murmur of voices at the entrance to the penthouse brought him upright.

One o'clock. It was about damn time she got in.

He pushed away from the desk and headed for the other room. He halted one step into the living room. Belle and Harry Walters were clearly silhouetted against the soft lights of the entrance, their shadows mingling with the sway of the ferns and ficus trees in the stir of air from the vent over their heads.

"That was lovely," Belle said softly. Her stance was relaxed, not poised for flight as it often seemed around him these days.

A hot wrench of emotion went through him. It wasn't jealousy, not at all. It was...concern. Harry was not the man for Belle. No way. Colt already had the two perfect candidates lined up. All she had to do was pick one.

"I thought so, too," Harry said in a husky tone, never taking his eyes off Belle. He put his arms around her.

Colt clenched his fists. The guy was all but drooling. The kiss started out light, but it progressed from there. Harry brought her closer. She let him. In fact, she reached up and laid her hand along Harry's cheek. But she didn't mold herself to him, Colt thought with a self-satisfied smirk. She didn't wrap her arms around him and ask him to show her what she was missing.

But she sure as hell was letting him kiss her and hold her a long time. Next thing he knew, they'd be on the sofa in a clinch.

He thought about punching Harry out. He thought about stuffing him into the trunk of his car and hauling him to the river and tossing him in. That would cool things down.... He realized he was the one popping out in a sweat.

Just when he could stand it no longer, the kiss ended.

"Will you be okay here alone?" Harry asked, concern in his voice.

Oh, yeah, as if she'd be safe for two seconds with lover boy staying over. Colt started to take a step forward.

"Of course. Thank you for sharing a wonderful evening with me."

"We could do it again," he suggested. He brushed the hair off her temple and let his finger trail down her cheek and across her lips.

Colt sizzled. He knew just how soft and expressive those lips could be. Harry bent and kissed her again, a quick kiss that spoke of his reluctance to leave. Belle saw him off, standing in the entrance and waving until the elevator door closed and hid his smile.

Colt walked back into the study and stood by the desk in the dark. When he heard Belle's steps in the hall, he reached over and flicked on the light.

He heard her gasp, then take a cautious step. Her head appeared in the open doorway.

"Oh, you scared me to death," she exclaimed, her tone not at all frightened.

But she should be. Colt saw red, literally, as he took in her appearance. She wore a red dress held up by two thin straps that wouldn't support a lace handkerchief. It stopped several inches short of her knees. He could see no lines under the red clingy stuff. She couldn't possibly be wearing a stitch of underclothes.

"Where did you get that dress?" he demanded, outraged that she would wear this dress for someone else...and he hadn't even seen it.

"At the store. You remember when you sent me to Kelley? She picked it out—"

"What were you trying to do—drive Harry right over the brink?" He could feel a vein pulsing in his neck and realized he was close to the exploding point. He drew a deep breath. Another. It didn't help.

"What are you talking about?"

"You," he thundered. "You're a walking invitation in that outfit."

She glanced down at her dress and shrugged. She slipped out of a pair of black sequined heels, scooped them up on two fingers and, with a yawn, waved good-night. She started down the hall.

It was too much. He went after her.

When his hand touched her shoulder—her bare, incredibly smooth shoulder—his anger transmogrified into something else, something less easy to define or control.

She faced him with a puzzled frown, then she said very softly, "Oh."

When he bent to her, Belle rose on her toes and met the kiss. She recognized the fury in him and knew it was composed of equal parts worry, frustration and hunger—that rapacious need that drove them into each other's arms at the slightest spark.

His hands moved over her. He wrapped her tighter and tighter in his embrace. His weight pressed her against the door frame, holding her captive to the kiss.

She felt a shudder go through him. It echoed in the depths of her being. The kiss was wild, almost as if they fought. She tossed her head restlessly. He ravaged her throat, found the slight dip between her breasts and licked her bare skin. His mouth moved to her breast and sucked at it through the soft material. She moaned as need too long suppressed shot through her.

"Colt, yes. Yes, darling, yes," she said over and over, hearing the desperation, the love she couldn't hide, in the words. It grew with each dazzling touch of his lips.

In one easy movement, he lifted her and went to his desk chair. There, he tucked her in his lap and leaned her back over his arm. Then he continued the wonder of his mouth on her, roaming over her face, her neck and down her chest.

He slipped one strap off her shoulder and discovered the bra cups tucked into her dress. With a wry smile, he laid them on the desk and proceeded in his ravishment.

She did her own exploring, sliding her hands under the soft cotton knit and rubbing all over his torso, absorbing the heat and wonder of him through her skin. At last she could stand it no longer.

"Take me to bed, Colt," she whispered. "Now. Please. Take me now."

He groaned, the sound deep in his throat, like that of a wounded animal too spent to move. "No," he said. "We have to save you for—"

"For?" she asked, kissing the beard-roughened jaw.

"For the husband you'll someday have."

She had no shield for her trembling emotions, not at this moment, not in his arms with his lips hot and wild on her. "I want you," she said raggedly. "Only you."

He raised his head. "The way you wanted Harry earlier?"

Colt heard himself ask the question and damned the part of him that had to say it. But he knew he had to put distance between them. The only way he could was with pain.

It appeared in her eyes as his meaning penetrated the foggy sensual haze surrounding them. Then it was gone, as if it had never been.

"I didn't want Harry. If I had, I'd have invited him to stay for a nightcap. And I would have been it."

The flippancy surprised him. Belle pushed against his shoulder and sat up. She lifted her straps into place, hiding the luxury of her breasts and their response to his touch. He almost groaned.

She peeled herself off him and stood, then she picked up the bra forms on the desk. He saw her pause and the frown deepen between her eyes. She bent and read the list he'd been working on earlier.

Belle read the names on the list. The two university guys—the Neanderthals—had had their names crossed out. Slocum's was also marked through. And two others. That left two names on the list. She went over the list of assets of each man, each listed in Colt's neat writing.

"What are these?" she asked.

He didn't answer, but she knew. She looked at the writing and the pencil on the desk. He'd been working on the list when she'd arrived home. "My marriage candidates," she said with a humorless smile. "You must be desperate to get rid of me."

Colt experienced the frustration of dealing with a female determined to be the injured party. "Dammit, Belle, things are getting out of hand between us. Hal is probably turning over in his grave now—"

"What has my father to do with it?"

"I promised him—" Colt stopped, but not in time. He saw the truth dawning in her eyes.

"He made you promise to marry me off to one of the blue bloods, didn't he? Too bad he didn't snap up one of the widows…or did he try that? Was he too rough and down-to-earth for their refined tastes? That's why I was sent to that fancy boarding school. So I would fit in."

"It wasn't like that—"

"Yes, it was. And you were part of it. Did he send you to me so you could talk me into sticking it out when I was so homesick I wanted to die?"

"No."

"Did he give you the list of acceptable names?" She gestured to the memo on the desk.

"I figured that out for myself," he admitted. If she wanted to be a martyr, he wouldn't stop her.

She walked away from him and stopped by the open door. "That's why you let me stay. Not to teach me the business, but to marry me off."

"You wouldn't make it in business. You're too soft," he told her bluntly.

She nodded. "You're right. I like people." She smiled, and the sadness showed through. "Most of them. Most of the time. I trusted you," she added, almost inaudibly. "I thought you were my friend."

"I am. That's why I was looking out for your best interests. You're ready for a home and family. I was trying to give you the best choices."

"You were trying to force me into accepting your choices. You know something, Colt? A benevolent dictator is still a dictator."

He rubbed the back of his neck, feeling the tension climb as she refused to listen to reason. "We'll talk about this tomorrow," he said. "It's late, and we're tired."

She nodded in agreement and left him.

Colt listened to her footsteps until she went into her room and closed the door. Tomorrow she would be more reasonable. She was angry with him now, but tomorrow she would see his side, understand that he had a promise to fulfill to her father and, more than that, he wanted only the best for her. Yeah, they would talk tomorrow.

But when he woke the next day, Belle was gone. He swore, then called Kelley.

"No, Belle isn't here. Is she supposed to be?" Kelley asked, puzzled by his call.

"No."

"Then why would you think she was here?"

The silence became overlong. "We had some words last night," he finally said. "She was gone when I woke up."

"Check with Carmen."

"Okay. Thanks."

"Call me if you don't find her soon."

He promised he would. After contacting Carmen, he called Leah, then Dee, then Mary, just on the off chance she might have gone over there. He even tried Pat at her new apartment. No one had heard from Belle.

She was doing this to drive him crazy, he decided after calling his ranch foreman and finding out for sure no one was at the main ranch house. It was working.

He talked to a cop friend after twenty-four hours.

"You say she packed all her clothes and took them?"

"Yeah."

"She's twenty?"

"Yes." Colt couldn't help the impatience.

"With no indication of foul play, there's not much we can do. She isn't exactly a teenage runaway," the cop said, his tone sympathetic. "You two have a lover's spat?"

"Hardly."

His friend chuckled. "Well, well, well. You've fallen at last. Welcome to the club. She'll turn up. Check with her friends."

"I've already called them," Colt said, his jaw so stiff he could hardly speak.

"Check with them tomorrow. She'll probably call. Hey, keep in touch, buddy. And invite me to the wedding." Still chortling over his humor, the cop hung up.

Colt jammed the phone down. He looked at the list of names on the incriminating memo Belle had seen. He looked at the requirements for her husband. So much for Plan B. He ripped the memo to confetti and let the pieces fall into the trash can.

For most of the day, he paced the floor, waiting for a call, for her to return, contrite and sorry....

At midnight, he admitted she wasn't coming back. If he ever found her he would...he would...kiss her senseless.

The truth hit him like a sledgehammer.

"My God," he said. His insides jumped around and got bent all out of shape. What a fool he'd been.

And Belle would be the first to tell him so. If he ever found her...no, not if, *when*...

He thought of all the things he should have done with her while she was there. He could have listened, no, *respected* her wishes and dreams. He and Hal had thought they were doing the best for Belle, but she'd been right. It was the best from their point of view, not hers.

Guilt pinged through him. It seemed to echo in the emptiness inside the condo. He cursed the list of marriage candidates and their qualifications. That had been a stupid thing to do…and it had hurt Belle.

Belle can do better'n a couple of roustabouts like us, eh, lad?

Bitter regret washed through Colt. He'd been so grateful to be a part of their family, so humble at being taken inside their closeness, that he'd believed Hal. He'd looked upon the older man as a hero, his mentor. He'd been awed when Hal had listened to his ideas and pooled his money with Colt's to develop the oil leases Colt had bought, ones that others thought were worthless.

And he'd believed it when Hal had said a roustabout wasn't good enough for Belle.

Okay, he didn't have a formal degree, but he hired people who did and he listened to their ideas and put them with his own until the company was as sound as any Fortune 500 business.

Texas blue blood? His family had been pioneers in Texas when it was still Mexican territory. An ancestor had been sent from the Alamo to get help. His folks had been ranchers and dirt farmers before any of the oil men had moved in and gotten rich off the land others had sweated their lives into. His parents hadn't been rich, but they'd been decent.

Who had equal wealth and didn't give a damn about her money? Who would be a good husband to her and loving father to her children? More important, who had the essential qualification above all others that he required in her mate—that of loving her more than life itself?

He did. Colt McKinnon, common roustabout.

He had loved her forever. He wanted only the best for her. He had cared about her and nurtured her and once...once he'd listened to her dreams. Until she'd learned she couldn't trust him with those dreams.

And then she'd left.

Belle had offered him her love with no holding back. But she had given up on him. Her leaving proved that. He'd had his chance to love and cherish her, to take all the warmth and cheer she lavished on those she cared for. He'd had that chance. He'd blown it.

For good?

No, he knew Belle. She had the most forgiving heart of any person alive. As soon as he found her, he'd explain how thickheaded he'd been. She'd forgive him, and all would be well. They'd live happily ever after, as all the fairy tales promised.

Chapter Ten

Belle inspected the neat apartment. It was actually one room with a tiny kitchen set into an alcove. The bathroom was next-door. A door set in the hallway gave her privacy from the rest of the house. The place was cheerful, with its pink and yellow rose-strewn wallpaper. She liked it.

"This will do fine," she told the elderly widow Mrs. Cummings who waited patiently for her decision.

"Mind, I don't hold with wild parties or drugs," the widow told her.

"I don't do either one," Belle assured the woman, a slight cynicism edging the words. She didn't do anything crazy, except fall in love with a man who wanted to get rid of her.

Her heart flip-flopped as it did each time she thought of Colt. Pushing aside his image from two weeks ago, she dug her checkbook out of her purse and paid the deposit and her first month's rent.

"May I move in today?" she asked.

"Yes, indeed." Mrs. Cummings deposited the check in her dress pocket. "You say you're a psychology student?"

"Yes. I'd like to go into family counseling, especially where children are involved."

"Well, I always thought that lack of family values was half the problem with kids nowadays."

"You may be right." Belle headed for the door. "I'll go get my things. I need a key."

"Oh, yes, I stuck it in my pocket." The widow fished it out and handed it over. "I'm sometimes forgetful. Well, at eighty-three, a person has a lot of memories cluttering up the brain." She grinned and her face crinkled into a thousand lines.

With her silver hair sticking out like a halo around her head and her merry ways, she reminded Belle of an elderly imp, bent on mischief still.

Belle smiled and wondered what her life would be like at eighty-three. What memories would she have? Would she have grandchildren, maybe great-grandchildren, by then?

She walked back to the tiny hotel she'd stayed in while she searched for an apartment she could afford, enrolled in the university and arranged to have a transcript of her grades sent to the registrar. With a place to live, she was all set. She'd even found a job.

An hour later, the cab driver helped her carry her bags into her new home. She paid him, then walked to the grocery a block away. She brought home milk, cereal, fruit, sandwich makings and three plants.

She placed a pot of tiny roses on the table in the alcove and the pots of vines on a windowsill and the coffee table. A daybed served as sleeping place and sofa. It had a deep green coverlet with pink and yellow stripes. Her mother would have liked the colors.

By the time Belle had unpacked and placed her personal belongings around the room, it felt like home. At four, she plopped down in a cushioned kitchen chair and ate a sandwich. She was tired, but it wasn't an unpleasant feeling. She'd accomplished what she set out to do when she slipped quietly out of Colt's home.

She now had a place of her own. If it seemed empty, she could live with that. She'd lived with other losses. She was at least standing on her own two feet, with neither Colt or the trust fund behind her as a safety net. She would study what interested her. If she failed, well, so be it.

At five, she dressed and went to work.

"Have you heard anything?" It was the first question Colt asked Carmen each morning when he arrived at the office. Not that he expected anything after three weeks.

"Yes."

He was halfway to his desk before her answer registered. He spun and returned to the door. "What?"

"Yes." His secretary smiled.

"Did she say where she was?"

Carmen held out a letter. An address he didn't recognize was in the left corner, but the writing was Belle's. His heart jumped to his throat in relief.

"About damn time," he muttered, and went to his desk to read it. His fingers trembled slightly when he drew the single sheet of paper from the envelope.

The letter was brief. She told him she had an apartment and a job and that she had enrolled in the university to study psychology and family counseling.

Colt nodded. Family counseling. Yeah, that suited her.

The relief disappeared when he skimmed through the last few lines.

> Since I'm not studying business as you and my father thought I should, I don't expect any aid from the trust fund. With my present job and my savings from working this summer, I have enough to make it for a year. I will apply for student loans to finish. Thank you for your help in teaching me about the holding company. Mostly I'm grateful because it gave me a chance to meet some wonderful people who are now my friends. Enclosed is the name of an attorney. He will represent me in our business dealings. I would rather not see you again. I hope you have a very happy life.
>
> Sincerely,
> Belle

He couldn't believe the letter. He studied the signature as if it might give him a clue to the person who wrote it. It didn't sound like Belle. Not *his* Belle.

She wasn't his, he reminded himself savagely. Whatever she'd once felt for him, it was evident she hated him now. He carefully returned the letter to the envelope and stored it in his desk. The phone rang. He grimly picked it up. There was work to be done.

* * *

"No, he never asks about her," Carmen said into the telephone. "Not since he got that letter. Whatever she said in it seemed to... Well, Colt is different."

"I'm worried," Kelley told her. "It's been two months. Belle doesn't mention Colt at all when we have lunch. It's as if she exists in a vacuum. She's charming and smiling, but nothing seems to touch her personally."

"Colt works twenty-four hours a day. If he isn't out on an oil rig, he's at one of the supply depots, checking delays and handling problems that he would ordinarily leave to the managers. He's lost weight."

"Hmm, I think it's time to call a meeting. I'll be seeing Mary this afternoon. Can you get hold of Leah and Dee? We'll work out a strategy."

"Good. Pat's our receptionist. I'll invite her. How about my place tomorrow night? We've got to work fast. Belle's birthday is Sunday."

Colt entered the office still in jeans and work boots on Friday morning. Oil stains covered his shirt.

Carmen spoke into the telephone. "In Belle's neighborhood? Just down the street? A drive-by shooting?"

He stopped abruptly. His heart kicked up into his throat. "What?" he asked. "What shooting?"

Carmen waved him off as she listened intently. Just as he was ready to snatch the receiver from her hand, she hung up. "It was nothing."

"A drive-by shooting in Belle's neighborhood? That's nothing? The place is probably crawling with pimps and drug runners—" Although it had looked fine when he'd driven by.

"It's a university neighborhood, mostly students," Carmen assured him. "It was probably a mistake about the shooting. Belle thinks it was a car backfiring and that the police are making too much of it. After all, there was only a little blood—"

"Blood," he repeated, seeing Belle lying on a cold sidewalk as her life ran out of her in a growing red tide.

"There was no body," Carmen said. "It might not have been blood. Belle said she didn't actually see any when she went to investigate—"

"She what?" Fury erupted in him, hot and heavy. It was just like Belle to risk her own life for a stranger.

"When she went out to investigate the drive-by shooting. Which was probably a car backfiring. She thinks."

Pat appeared in the doorway to the receptionist's area. "You know, when I was living on the street, I saw some man shoot another. Blood flew all over the storefront. It was a robbery in that market down near the park where I used to live—"

"My God," Colt said. He could feel the blood pooling inside him, flowing into some abyss that dropped straight down into the bowels of hell.

The phone rang and Pat went to answer it. Carmen studied him, an anxious expression in her eyes. "Do you think Belle is okay in that neighborhood? She assured me it was perfectly safe. She said no one has bothered her at all when she walks home from the restaurant at midnight."

"Midnight," he repeated in a near roar. "Of all the lamebrain— Honest to pete, she hasn't a lick of— I ought to—'' He slammed the heel of his hand against the door frame. "I'll check out the place," he told Carmen. "You can stop worrying. If it isn't a safe neighborhood, she'll be back in the condo so fast, it'll make her head swim."

"Hurry," Carmen advised. "She'll be twenty-one Sunday. Then you won't have any authority."

Colt stared at her. He hadn't thought of that. Well, it didn't matter. He wasn't going to stand by and see Belle get hurt. She would just have to get over this idiotic flight of independence or whatever it was.

He managed to get a modicum of work done that day.

At five, before she left the office, Carmen asked, "What are you going to do about Belle?" she asked, her eyes kind. "You will be careful and not hurt her feelings, won't you? She's more sensitive than she lets on."

"I should never have let her go off on her own," he admitted. "I didn't realize..."

"That you were madly in love with her?"

He felt a flush start in the center of his chest and work its way to his face. He stared into her sympathetic gaze, then sighed in defeat. "Is it that obvious?"

"Only that you're worried about her."

"If I'd known it sooner—" He shook his head. "She had to leave before it hit me. I realized lots of things when she walked out."

"Such as the fact that Belle has grown up?"

He flashed Carmen a troubled glance.

"I noticed, for all her sparkle and flash, that she was more mature than my own daughter. It was to be expected, I suppose. She lost her mother at an early age. She was sent away from her home. She's traveled the world. Then she lost her father. Those are life experiences, and they change the person who goes through them.''

"She was too young at seventeen,'' he said, old memories crowding in.

"But not at twenty-one.''

"I'm nearly fourteen years older.''

"In your heart, Colt, does that matter?''

"Not to me, but she's young. She deserves someone as idealistic as she is.''

"She deserves a man who will love and cherish her all her life.'' Carmen smiled. "Belle loves flowers.''

Belle finished blow-drying her hair. She slipped into the shorts that went with her outfit, tucked in the white blouse, added the formal jacket and clipped the little black bow tie under the collar of the blouse. She put on the rather thick makeup the owner liked for the waitresses to wear. The mascara made her eyes look bigger. She finished and went to collect the rest of her things.

Someone knocked on the door.

Startled, she dropped the silly pillbox hat she had to wear with her uniform and stuck her eye close to the peephole in the door. She gasped, stepped back and stared as if the door might burst from its hinges at any second.

"Belle?''

Taking a breath, she pulled open the door. "Colt, hello. What are you doing here?''

"I was in the neighborhood." He handed her a pot of tiny pink roses and stepped inside.

She closed the door and looked around, then finally set the flowerpot on the coffee table. "You were in the neighborhood."

"I came to see you."

He strolled around the tiny apartment, stopping to peer at various objects, one of them being the picture she always carried with her. It was of him and her dad standing by their first oil rig. Another was of her and her mother.

"Nice place," he commented.

"Thank you."

"Got a cup of coffee? It's been miserable drinking my own brew after getting used to yours."

"You grind the grounds too fine, and you use too much."

"I knew something was wrong."

She was puzzled by the odd conversation. "I can make a fresh pot." She did so, sneaking a glance at her watch to check the time. "I have to leave for work in a half hour."

"I'll drive you down," he promised. "Kelley said you were working at the seafood place near the river."

"Yes. It's nice. My boss is nice. And the other waitresses." She sounded like a ninny.

"Good." He helped himself to coffee when the pot stopped gurgling. "You want some?"

She nodded and sat at the kitchen table. He handed her a cup. Her fingers tingled unbearably when his lightly touched hers in the exchange. He sat opposite her.

"How are your classes going?" he asked.

"Fine."

"What time do you get off work?"

"Midnight."

"You walk home?"

"It isn't far," she said quickly. To her surprise, he didn't frown or give her a lecture about it. Under his prodding, she told him about her teachers, the people she worked with and her landlady.

"What about the shooting?"

She looked at him blankly. "What shooting?"

"The one here in the neighborhood, the one you went to investigate."

"There hasn't been any shooting that I know of. This is a very quiet neighborhood, families and students mostly."

"Hmm."

A smile curled the corners of his mouth, and her heart did a funny, little achy hitch. He pushed at the lock of dark hair that arched over his forehead. It sprang back into place. Sometimes he could look so endearing. She looked away before she did something stupid...such as fall at his feet and tell him how much she missed him.

Living with him had been a mistake. It made being alone that much harder to bear.

Finally she glanced at her watch again. "I've got to go to work."

He drove her down and gave her a friendly wave when she hopped out. Going inside, she tried to assess the half hour, but couldn't decide what his attitude had been. He had observed her with a...a quiet look in his eyes, maybe even tenderness—

No, she was getting fanciful. He was merely checking up on her. After all, he was still her guardian. For—she looked at the clock when she went into the restaurant—for six more hours. Then he wouldn't have to see her again.

Colt realized he was nervous. More than that. He was terrified. Confronting Belle wasn't like hanging on to an oil derrick four or five stories off the ground and getting washed down by a geyser of black gold, all the while knowing a slip could be the end of it. No, Belle was more dangerous.

She came out of the restaurant at fifteen minutes after midnight. It was now Sunday morning.

"Belle," he called before she turned up the street.

She paused and stared at the parking lot. "Colt?"

"Yeah. You want a ride home?"

"I...thank you." She hurried across the dark patch of lawn and got into his car.

He put it in gear and headed for her place, which was only two blocks away. He noted the streets were well lit. He drove past a grocery which stayed open twenty-four hours a day. There were people going in and out.

"Looks like a family-oriented neighborhood," he said as the silence grew between them.

At her house, she paused with her hand on the door handle and frowned at him, obviously not sure what to do.

"Invite me in for a nightcap," he suggested. He barely suppressed a grin and wondered if she remembered referring to herself as a nightcap the night she went out with Harry.

He did, and he'd thought about having her since.

The startled glance she shot him convinced him she recalled the flippant remark, too. Good. That would give her something to think about.

Once they were inside, she put on the coffee, using decaffeinated, he noticed, then excused herself. Taking a pair of sweats with her, she went into the bathroom. He prowled the apartment, again stopping in front of the two pictures on a side table. He'd been around twenty-one when Lily had snapped the one of him and her father. She'd been ten in the one with her mother.

She returned, dressed in the dark blue sweats, her face scrubbed clean of the makeup she'd worn earlier. He liked her better like this. He watched her pour two mugs of coffee, then he joined her at the apartment-size table.

"This is a cozy place."

"Yes. I was lucky to find it."

"So you said. I hope you aren't going to miss it too much." He smiled when she looked puzzled and moved his chair to one side so he could stretch his legs out. "When you move back to the condo."

Twin flags of anger appeared in her cheeks. Ah, the old Belle wasn't completely gone.

"I'm not moving back," she said, her lips tucked into stubborn lines.

He set his cup down and leaned toward her. "I think you should."

"Well, I don't." She glared at him.

"I miss your singing in the shower."

"Ha."

"Also the dinners you used to prepare. The biscuits, too. They sure were good, especially with chicken-fried steak and mashed potatoes. I miss the way you lectured me on my love life. You were right. I would never have been happy with someone like Marsha.''

She stared into her coffee cup, a flicker of emotion running over her face, but too fast for him to read.

"What are you talking about?"

"Me. You. Us."

That brought her gaze back to him. "It's late," she said. "We're both probably tired. I think you should leave."

He shook his head. "Not without you."

She took a deep breath as if she sought control. He didn't want her to be calm. He wanted passion and fire and a need that outshone all else.

"Why are you doing this?" she asked.

He stood and came around the small table. "Because, to put it quite simply, I find I can't live without you."

Belle jumped to her feet and backed away when Colt reached for her. He followed, an odd light in his dark gray eyes, that little smile still curled into the corners of his mouth. She shook her head.

"That's absurd. You've never needed anyone."

"Not true. I thought I couldn't have you, that I wasn't good enough—"

"Why would you think that?" She was so choked and breathless, she could hardly get the words out. She wasn't even certain she was hearing correctly.

He walked forward until he had her trapped against the cabinet. An urge to flee grabbed her. She pressed her hands flat on the counter at each side of her. Colt placed his hands on the counter, too, his forearms touching her on each side.

"Someday I'll tell you," he said. "I'm thirteen years older than you. Does that bother you?"

She shook her head.

"Good." He dropped to one knee.

Belle stared at him. "What are you doing?"

"Proposing. Are you ready?"

"No," she yelped. She tried to dodge to the side, but he caught her easily.

"Stay put," he ordered. He reached into his jacket pocket and removed a jewelery box.

Her heart nearly beat its way out of her chest. She could only stare when he opened it. The diamond wasn't three carats, she thought inanely.

"This is a different ring," he explained. "It's not as large as the other—not quite two carats—but the stone is nearly flawless. I wanted one as perfect as possible."

He removed it from the box and held it out to her. She shied away, not certain what was going on. He clasped her hand in his. His felt warm. Hers was icy cold.

"Will you marry me, Belle? I promise to be a loving husband to you and a good father to our children."

"Why?" she asked.

"Because I love you. I always have. I suspect I always will." He gave her a rueful grin. "It's just that I have this thick head. It takes a while for me to catch on to things...like love, like life, like...forever."

Belle saw herself reflected in his dark gaze. She

looked dazzled and somewhat uncertain. But that's what life did to a person—knocked you around a bit, then just when you decided to grow up and accept that there weren't any fairy godmothers, it tossed your wildest dream into your lap.

He slipped the ring on her finger. It fit perfectly. "Say something," he ordered. "Say yes."

"Yes." She threw her arms around him and squeezed him for all she was worth, with all the love that had always lived in her heart for him, for this one man. "Oh, yes."

Then he kissed her, and all the world stood still. It was wonderful and satisfying...well, kind of...

"More," she whispered when they came up for air. "Show me everything."

"Not tonight." He looked a bit shaken. "We're not going—"

"I know the rest of that one," she interrupted, her heart turning cartwheels.

He drew a careful breath and held her hands away from him when she would have caressed him some more. "Cut that out...until we're married," he added huskily.

"Let's elope."

"How about a Christmas wedding? We'll have a couple of weeks for a honeymoon. I find I want you all to myself for a nice long stretch of time."

She shivered at the look in his eyes. He drew her with him to the chair. Sitting with her in his lap, they planned a rosy future. "When the alarm clock goes off, and I wake and find I dreamed all this, I'll die," she murmured, kissing along his neck.

"It's no dream."

A car horn sounded in the distance. "I'll need a car to drive to school after we're married. Your place isn't close enough to walk."

"I'll get you one for Christmas."

"My father said I was the worst driver in the state of Texas," she warned him, trying to be fair and honest about her shortcomings.

Colt laughed softly. "I know for a fact your dad was sometimes wrong."

"Like he was wrong in his choices for me?"

Colt realized she had intuitively figured out why he could never admit the possibility of loving her as more than the child he had watched grow into womanhood. "Yes, we were both wrong there. You were right." He gave her a wry grin as he admitted it.

"Well," she said, turning her most earnest expression on him, her eyes dancing. "I am an excellent judge of character, you know."

Epilogue

"Belle, you look beautiful, just radiant." Kelley smoothed a ruffle of white silk, then stood back to admire the effect. She clapped her hands. "Okay, bridesmaids to this side, groomsmen over here. Let's get this finished. The guests are waiting."

Belle felt radiant. This was her wedding day, her dream-come-true day. She looked at her brand-new husband. He glanced at her at that moment. His gaze swept over her in one quick, all-encompassing perusal that seared right down to the cockles of her heart, wherever those were.

She suppressed the bubble of laughter that rose to her throat. She should be properly subdued and elegant on her wedding day, she chided her giddy spirit. Except she felt she'd gotten the last laugh on life.

"Smile," Kelley ordered.

The photographer snapped picture after picture. For an instant, Belle felt regret that neither Colt's nor her parents were there to see their happiness.

"Now one of Belle, Carmen, Mary, Dee and me," Kelley dictated, obviously in her element. She'd helped Belle plan the color scheme, using the holiday colors.

Belle had considered getting married in red silk, which was the color of good luck in Asian weddings, but her friends had insisted on white.

"After all," Kelley had said, "you're the only one of us who can wear white in the traditional sense."

Belle had given her friends a mischievous glance. "You don't know that," she'd murmured. Then she'd giggled and spoiled the effect.

A shiver of anticipation ran over her. *Tonight.*

Colt touched her shoulder lightly, then stepped away so her bridesmaids could crowd around her. She smiled and smiled all afternoon. Finally, after dark settled over the town, after the dinner was eaten and the toasts were raised to the couple, Colt turned to her. "Ready to go?"

She nodded.

He had planned to take her to Hawaii, but she'd vetoed that idea. She knew exactly where she wanted to spend her wedding night. They changed to jeans and shirts, each in a separate room at the church, and, amid a shower of birdseed, headed for the ranch. Belle wanted to spend the first night of her marriage in the house where they would live most of the time once they had children. She and Colt had already agreed on that.

She sighed happily. Her life was on track.

At the ranch he left her at the house while he murmured about checking on something. Belle changed into the nightgown her bridesmaids had presented to her. Then, trying to decide whether she was nervous or not, or whether she should be nervous or not, she slipped into the bed and waited. But not for long.

She heard his step in the hallway, then the door opened. Colt came in. He was barefoot as always in the house. He sat down beside her. "How sleepy are you at the moment?"

"Very." She held the smile in.

"Hmm." He gave her a kiss, then settled beside her, his arm protectively over her waist.

She waited. He simply held her. She cleared her throat. He patted her arm. She noticed the smile lurking at the corners of his mouth.

"When does the ravishment start?" she demanded.

He raised his head. "I read this book about virgins and wedding nights. It said I should give you time to get used to me." He snuggled close. "In fact, it advised resting the first night—"

"After all the years I've waited for you? No way."

If he wouldn't begin the fireworks, she would. First she kissed him along his jaw, then softly on his mouth, then, opening his shirt, across his chest. She nuzzled her nose into the ticklish hairs there and licked his skin.

Soon she decided that wasn't enough. She tugged apart the snap on his jeans, then unzipped them. He opened his eyes.

"You would be more comfortable without these," she suggested in sultry tones.

"I think you're right," he agreed. He shucked them off.

She snuggled up to him. "I'm going to kiss you for a while. Just to let you get used to me." She proceeded to ravish him, very lavishly and very thoroughly.

Colt let her explore for five, ten, fifteen minutes. It was the sweetest torture he could imagine.

Sweat broke out all over him. He wanted Belle to be thoroughly comfortable with his body before he proceeded. He'd give her another few minutes...another couple of minutes...

"That's it," he muttered when her explorations grew too intimate. He rolled over, balancing his weight on his elbows as he looked down at his beautiful wife. He trembled with the love he felt for her. Tonight would be the first time for them, but he would never tire of making love to her in a hundred years...or of being with her.

She made each day an adventure. She was forever bringing something new into their lives—usually people she met. She showered her warmth and humor on everyone, but to him, she gave the most—her incredible faith, her unwavering love and, tonight, everything else.

"Let's get these out of the way," he suggested, his voice husky with the desire he didn't try to hide. He reached for the silky material of her gown.

She laid a hand over his. "Darling, you know the rule."

He paused and tried to think of something he had left out. "I have protection," he assured her.

"Not that." Her slow smile lit up her face. "It's the one about the waist."

"The waist?"

"Well, just my waist, I suppose."

She touched him in an intimate fashion, making his

heart—and other parts—jump. When he saw the gleam in her eyes, he suppressed a smile and gave her a stern glare. "Belle, what are you trying to say?"

"No going below the waist." She slapped his hand. "That's the rule. You made it yourself."

He uttered a low growl of laughter. "It's one I'm going to have to break. You've worn my resistance down to nothing. I can't seem to keep my hands off you."

He demonstrated what he meant.

"Well," she drawled when they came up for air, "I'm sure...pretty sure...not one hundred percent, mind you, but I *think* your intentions are honorable. After all, I am an excell...mmm...mmm..mmm..."

* * * * *

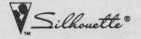

Take 2 bestselling love stories FREE

Plus get a FREE surprise gift!

Special Limited-Time Offer

Mail to Silhouette Reader Service™

3010 Walden Avenue
P.O. Box 1867
Buffalo, N.Y. 14240-1867

YES! Please send me 2 free Silhouette Romance™ novels and my free surprise gift. Then send me 6 brand-new novels every month, which I will receive months before they appear in bookstores. Bill me at the low price of $2.90 each plus 25¢ delivery and applicable sales tax, if any.* That's the complete price, and a saving of over 10% off the cover prices—quite a bargain! I understand that accepting the books and gift places me under no obligation ever to buy any books. I can always return a shipment and cancel at any time. Even if I never buy another book from Silhouette, the 2 free books and the surprise gift are mine to keep forever.

215 SEN CH7S

Name	(PLEASE PRINT)	
Address	Apt. No.	
City	State	Zip

This offer is limited to one order per household and not valid to present Silhouette Romance™ subscribers. *Terms and prices are subject to change without notice. Sales tax applicable in N.Y.

USROM-98   ©1990 Harlequin Enterprises Limited

Silhouette Romance
celebrates the joys
of first love in
VIRGIN BRIDES

September 1998:
THE GUARDIAN'S BRIDE
by Laurie Paige (#1318)
A young heiress, desperately in love with her
older, wealthy guardian, dreams of wedding the
tender tycoon. But he has plans to marry
her off to another....

October 1998:
THE NINE-MONTH BRIDE
by Judy Christenberry (#1324)
A widowed rancher who wants an heir and a prim librarian
who wants a baby decide to marry for convenience—but will
motherhood make this man and wife rethink their
temporary vows?

November 1998:
A BRIDE TO HONOR by Arlene James (#1330)
A pretty party planner falls for a charming, honor-bound
millionaire who's being roped into a loveless marriage. When
the wedding day arrives, will *she* be his blushing bride?

December 1998:
A KISS, A KID AND A MISTLETOE BRIDE (#1336)
When a scandalous single dad returns home at
Christmas, he encounters the golden girl he'd fallen
for one magical night a lifetime before.

Available at your favorite retail outlet.

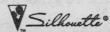

Silhouette®

Look us up on-line at: http://www.romance.net   SRVBSD

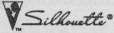

Silhouette ROMANCE™

COMING NEXT MONTH